Murder
in
St. Michaels

Murder in St. Michaels

Marci Lynn McGuinness

ISBN: 0-938833-46-4
ISBN-13: 978-0938833-46-8

Published by: Shore Publications
P. O. Box 111, Chalk Hill, PA 15421

www.ohiopyle.info
www.uniontownspeedway.com
www.amazon.com/author/marcimcguinness

DEDICATION

This book is dedicated to all mystery writers,
especially my hero, Agatha Christie.

I also want to thank the many Eastern and Western Shore folks
who I got to know during my 5 year stay "On the Shore."

ACKNOWLEDGMENTS

I spent 5 years on the Eastern Shore of Maryland living in Tilghman, St. Michaels, and Chestertown. My column, *On the Shore with Marci* in *Spin Sheet* magazine of Annapolis, took me to islands and coves and boat building shacks. I interviewed characters whose families had lived on the shore for many generations.

I belonged to the Miles River Yacht Club and was the Managing Editor of Tidewater Publishers/Cornell Maritime Press in Centreville. Publishing articles and books on the Chesapeake Bay and Maritime Industries put me in contact with the real people and culture of both shores. For this, I am deeply grateful.

CHAPTER 1

"Goodbye Youghiogheny River," I yelled, listening to the echo bounce off Kentuck Mountain. Glancing at the Ferncliff Peninsula one last time, I poised on tip-toes above the Ohiopyle Falls, fingertips reaching to the clear Indian-summer sky. Taking a deep breath I sprung up, over and into deep chilling frothy white water. A cold shock jolted me for a long moment. The bubbly, rushing water enveloped my body, pushing me to the surface like it had so many times these past forty years, with the love and knowledge that I'd be back another day to say a final goodbye with my ashes.

I climbed up the familiar sand-gray river rocks throwing dark wet hair back from my smiling face, remembering my first falls-dive. I was upset with Mom and Dad. My uncle, who adored his little sister, asked me to take a walk with him. I had always felt a special kinship between us even as a little girl, but as I grew and looking back, I realize it was our likeness that drew us together. He always knew when I was feeling low. This particular evening we ended up at the top of the falls. He told me a story about him and his buddies when they were my age, which was 17 then. Seems they had many a party on the flat rocks overlooking the rushing waters. "Follow me," was all he said. It was the look in his eyes that gave me the courage to run behind him and dive that summer. Every once in a while throughout my lifetime when I feel so intensely emotional that I think I'll pop, I take the leap, thanking him for the gift.

As I climbed up the rocky bank, my Blue Tick Hound, Hank, joined me, jumping and barking. Ranger Dick Humbert pulled along my side in his park-issued Ford® Bronco just as we stepped onto the falls overlook parking lot. A few of the rangers in Ohiopyle State Park in southwestern Pennsylvania were forever trying to catch the locals diving or running kayaks over the falls. The fine was overblown, but they rarely got there in time to actually see anyone in action. For all he knew, I had been swimming above the falls area.

"I know what you did," he sneered.

"That's nice." I broke into a sprint, and waved as I left him there grumbling, rolling a wooden toothpick in his mouth through the gap between his front teeth.

"And get that mangy dog on a leash or I'll sure cite you!" he yelled after us. I turned and threw him a kiss. Kissed the jerk goodbye, I suppose. Made his day-his year-no doubt. I had held a grudge against the not-so-bright ranger since the day they found Willie buried in the park. There was something in his eyes that told me he was laughing at me. Enjoying my grief and pain.

I had dreamed of leaving home for the last couple of years. Life without Willie here was smothering me. Reading about the Chesapeake Bay's Eastern Shore, and listening to fishing stories at my general store and diner from regulars who go there, raised my curiosity. After my son, Willie, came up missing and was found buried in the park, my love of these mountains melted away like snow banks in the spring. When I finally put the Ohiopyle Company Store, apartment and all, on the market, it sold within weeks.   It was my turn to go where I needed to be. To make my way in unknown territory.

When I handed the keys over to the couple who bought the old brick store, my feet froze to the ground. My head spun, stomach muscles clenched. I slowly looked to the sky, taking in deep breaths and knew I was doing the right thing. I needed this break to survive and grow. After looking around at the mountains that had protected me, but not my sweet boy, I jumped in the van with Hank and shook the tears away. He licked my face, conveying that it would be alright. He woofed and looked toward the road. Let's go, he was telling me. It's time now. Another deep breath, a change of gears, and we pulled away from our old life, friends waving from the Liar's Bench on the front porch.

Tears choked me most of the way, interspersed by singing and hysterical laughter. Hank smiled and nudged me with his head, licked my shoulder, then my arm. Seemed to want me to be alright with the decision to go.

Dogs are so very wise that way. They have instincts humans only pray they can achieve. With the sun roof open, I felt like a kid embarking on a scary, but necessary adventure. I had written a few booklets on local folklore, history, tourism, fishing, and hunting. I had supported my son and worked from dawn till dusk in the store and diner. Hauled his friends to all the football and baseball games. Dealt with teachers good and not so great.

It took us about three hours to get to Annapolis. So many thoughts streamed through my mind. I repeatedly shook my head in order to concentrate on driving, like a trucker falling asleep at the wheel, but I was far from napping. At Keyser's Ridge I had left Route 40 and turned west on Route 68. Our first stop was the Prime Outlets in Hagerstown. New jeans for me and a classy collar for Hank made us both smile.

The Maryland state capital was fun for a couple days stay. I shot fresh oyster shooters at a couple sailor's taverns, and walked the docks taking in the yachts, race boats, and navy vessels. But the Bay Bridge was calling my name, screaming it, really, and I needed to answer it. To see what was on the other side.

The Chesapeake Bay Bridge toll gate man smiled while handing me change for $5. I dropped it in the ash try of the old station wagon, and got in the right lane so I could watch the sail boats as I made my way to the "Land of Pleasant Living."

"Hello Chesapeake Bay!" I yelled.

Sails spotted the water. A tug boat slowly hauled an enormous barge and its cargo. Condos and restaurants lined the shore. Four miles of bridge landed me on Kent Island. The wind and semi salty air filled my heart, a heart struggling to be free. I felt my spirits begin to lift. Shoulders loosened. I was going home, but knew no one and had no idea where I would work. Hank, Willie's Blue Tick Hound, watched out the window, grinning. He loves warm air. Hated the snows in Pennsylvania. So did I, but Willie had loved it there and would have never agreed to move away. He refused to leave his friends when I had it all set up for us to move to a brownstone in Queens, New York. He was in the seventh grade then, a year before his murder. Everyone had told me the big city was a dangerous place to take a young boy. I have learned that no place is safe.

I wanted to write and make my mark on the world outside the confines of the Allegheny Mountains. My freedom to do this was a long time coming. Running the business and bringing up Willie took all my strength. Then discovering and dealing with his killer knocked me down for a long time. But this was a new day, a new time. I was dying for fresh experiences and a more detached life. No one knew me here. No sad looks, odd verbal exchanges about how I must be coping, and no one staring at me when they think I am not noticing.

With my old Steelers cap on my head – it had belonged to Willie's dad before the accident took him away from us – I hoped for good luck now. It was time it brought me some better luck. I just couldn't part with it. Always made me smile deep into my heart to think of Rusty jumping up and down, throwing this hat in the air while watching the Pittsburgh Steelers go for another touchdown.

I drove with all the windows down, getting butterflies in my stomach crossing the Oak Creek Bridge to St. Michaels.

"This place is adorable," I told Hank as we creeped through town obeying the 25 mph speed limit.

I had read about it and liked what I read, so I lined up a roommate situation to get me started. Iris Jenkins seemed very amiable on the phone and her e mails were encouraging. She owned a popular crab house. Chesapeake Bay Blue Crabs were big on the "shore." Hell, it was fall, and 75 degrees. My luck was on an upswing already.

Starved, I parked behind Poppi's Restaurant and entered the diner, purchasing the *Star Democrat* newspaper from the stand out front. It was 2pm. Lunch was ending. I had the place to myself except for a couple of old fellows at the counter. They both nodded their capped heads my way.

"Afternoon, fellas," I nodded in return.

After using the co-ed restroom, and combing water through my hair to get rid of the hat-hair look, I stretched and took a seat in a corner booth. As I opened the newspaper, a blonde waitress bounced my way. Alice was about my age with frizzy hair and a big welcome. She let me know that they only had one lunch special left, a crab cake sandwich with Cole slaw and hush puppies. I bit.

Willie and I were always eating together. It was

important to us that we had our little family dinner everyday. We'd spend over an hour sitting there talking and laughing. On weekends it was a huge breakfast that brought us to the kitchen enjoying buckwheat cakes, fresh local sausage, and home fries. These were the times that built our love and respect for each other. That thickened our bond as mother and son and friends for what turned out to be much too short a life together. I miss eating with Willie every time I sit down at a table.

Skimming the classifieds, one ad jumped out at me. "A rare opportunity" (it claimed) - busy waterside restaurant in need of a responsible service bar tender. Experienced only need apply. During the last twenty years I had waited on probably a million people in that diner I called home. We catered hundreds of parties and meetings, many at a nearby winery. Experience I had. References, no problem. I gobbled a succulent crab cake and went to the restroom to brush my teeth and hair. According to Alice, the Town Dock Restaurant was only a few blocks away.

Hank and I walked through the little town. Talbot Street was lined with turn of the century clapboard storefronts painted in bright colors. Gift shops, gourmet chocolates and picnic lunches here, homemade ice cream there, top of the line clothiers, books, hats, a few taverns and restaurants; so quaint. I turned just past the Post Office and found the Town Dock Restaurant right on the water. Harbor views, cruisers galore.

I tied Hank to a small tree and opened the double doors. Luckily, the owner and manager were at the hostess desk having a conversation. Sammy introduced himself as the Chef and proprietor, and Todd as one of the dining room managers. What a breathtaking panoramic view of St. Michaels Harbor, glistening blue water lapping, a myriad of boats moving along, docked. This was all glassed in with several levels of deck seating. All in all, over 200 could dine comfortably, I figured. Waitresses ran from the swinging kitchen doors, down several levels of steps with overloaded trays of seafood. They were busy even after lunch and this was a weekday in September. A good sign. I could see the service bar also had a few stools for guests to sit before dinner. I talked with the fellows, gave them the rundown of my experience and situation, and filled out an application. By the way they looked at me, both smiling, I knew I was in. They said most of their summer help went back to college and they were in need of someone reliable immediately. I told them I'd be available to start the next day. As Hank and I walked back through town, I got myself a Post Office box and, wala, I was a resident of St. Michaels, Maryland.

Now, to find my new home. Iris Jennings said it would be alright to have a dog, but she had never lived with a howling hound born to hunt. He would kill and maim unsuspecting birds and small animals if I didn't keep a good rein on him. I could not let him run free here like he was used to doing in the mountains, but he would adjust. Luckily, she didn't have a canary.

Iris had sent me directions in an e mail. She lived just off of Railroad Avenue. I had passed the turn when I went to Poppi's. There were a few interesting shops on the corner that I knew I'd later explore. Chesapeake Outfitters, Flamingo Flats, Justine's Ice Cream Shop, Chesapeake Bay Trading Post. Maybe I'd get a new look to celebrate my new life.

As I passed the offices for the Chesapeake Bay Maritime Museum, I spotted it. The brick two story cape style home was caressed by huge willow trees on either side of the walkway flanked by a double garage and in-ground pool. Iris had been widowed, too, a few years back, was around my age, I think, and advertised for a roommate at this time to bring some life back into her home. Good company I could handle. It had been over three years since Willie died. I had been alone long enough.

A deep bark welcomed us. It was Iris' Newfoundland, Ralph. His huge black hairy head took up most of the front window next to the door. We could see from the car that the wrap around porch held sturdy wicker furniture with bright colored pillows, a swing, a glider, and a huge dining table. I had always wanted a wrap around porch. My grandmother had one at the old hotel she ran when I was a little girl. I had loved playing there. It was after 3pm, so I hoped my new landlord would be home. She said she usually worked from 5am to 2:30pm and went back in the evening to close up. Sure enough she was coming out the door as we exited the Subaru®. What a smile. Long strides brought the auburn haired Iris to us in short order.

She grasped my shoulders and said, "Welcome to St. Michaels, Cedar Jace. I hope you will be as happy here as I have been."

Ralph leaped at Hank who in turn barked as if he was about to be eaten. He hopped around the big furry guy and they sniffed each other a minute or two. That was that. They were friends. Dogs! I kept him on a leash, though. One whiff of a neighbor's pet bird and that welcome could dry up in a Chesapeake Bay minute. No reason to ruin my new life so soon.

"Come on in. We can get your things in a bit. Allow me to show you around." Iris hugged me. I found that sweet and it took me off balance. A stranger, a hugger. Her eyes said she was happy to be the hostess.

Up the four wide steps we went. She laughed as she watched the dogs getting acquainted. "Ralph needs a friend to keep him in line. He is very spoiled, but good-natured."

"Hank is bit spoiled, too," I admitted.

It was lovely, comfortable, stylish. A gourmet kitchen was set up with a large chopping block/table in the center. Gleaming pots and skillets hung from an overhead rack. Navy marble counters shined, and a half bushel of Maryland blue crabs were sitting noisily in the sink.

"We'll have those fellas later. I brought them from work. They're jumbos. I knew we wouldn't be able to eat them all, so I invited a good friend to join us. You'll love Marley. She's a fire-woman here." Iris held up her hands and laughed. "She does a great job for them. Was actually the first one on the scene when my crab house caught on fire. Saved it single-handedly waiting for the guys to show up. I will always owe her for that. She is very strong inside and out, dedicated to her work and her friends." She paused and opened the door at the top of the stairs as I looked over the many photographs hanging along the stairway wall. There must have been thirty of them. Old family shots, I assumed, several handsome men. I made a mental note to ask about them later.

"You will have the second floor to yourselves. There is a back stairway off the balcony facing the pool area that leads to the driveway. Come on, let me show you to your parlor," she laughed. "I've always wanted to say that!"

I knew right then that I was a lucky girl gazing at my new accommodations. There was a bedroom and full bath. The living area overlooked the deck and pool. Hardwood floors, a huge desk, overstuffed sofa and chair, a rocker, and a thick center rug made me sigh. I was home.

"I think I can live with this," I told her, dropping my purse on a tall oak dresser. I had mailed her two months rent with the signed lease and photos of us. Told her that I would get work as soon as I got there, but had enough savings to keep me going for several months. My friends had a going away party for me--a surprise. Didn't seem to want me to go. It wasn't easy leaving all of them, but necessary to keep my sanity and get on to the next level of my existence. I wanted to live away from sorrowful eyes pitying me. Away from the burden of living across the road from where my son was killed and buried until discovered. Far away from the memories of discovering my own employee had poisoned my sweet boy.

Both dogs started barking. "That would be Marley. Let

me introduce you two then you can get settled while we get the crabs ready."

"Sounds like heaven to me." My mind was whirling.

Marley Landslide had Hank licking her face and Ralph woofing at her when we entered the kitchen. Her dark eyes looked deep into mine. I knew I was being checked out, but didn't mind. A careful suspicious person, this Marley. Like me.

"Cedar, I'm Marley. Welcome to the Eastern Shore." She shook my hand with a firm grasp and I took to her instantly. "This must be Hank. Iris mentioned Ralph was also getting a roommate. What a cool roughneck. Not many Blue Tick Hounds around here. He'll stand out in a crowd. Love those ears and eyes!"

"How about a beer you two?" our hostess offered.

"Beer sounds great," Marley said, cropped blonde hair framing her sculpted face.

CHAPTER 2

I shot out of bed and onto the deck at exactly 3:26 am,
according to the bedside clock. A fire alarm shrilled the
night air. "Where the hell am I?" was my first thought. I
held my head until it all came back. Hank was howling at
the sliding glass door. From my view I could see fire trucks
going south. It sounded like they stopped close-by, though.
Black smoke billowed up into the cool night sky. Hank and
Ralph howled in unison now, relentlessly. The front screen
door banged and a sleek figure in a flowing nightdress ran
down the road, bare feet slapping the pavement. I threw on
my favorite hoodie and ran to the front door, grabbed a
sweater from the hook there, and followed Iris' lead. At
dinner the ladies had clued me in about the people here. It
was so interesting listening to locals talk about locals. Very
much like my home in the mountains. Lots of gossip and
opinions. They had also mentioned, trying hard not to
alarm me, that a few arson-fires had been happening lately
and that people were both angry and afraid. This one was

only two blocks away-- Iris' Crab House.

"They got me this time," she stated when I approached. "They got me good."

I didn't know what to say, so I just wrapped the sweater around her shoulders. Her freckled face glowed in the firelight. Green eyes sharp. Hair blowing back. Tears streaming.

The smell of charred crab, oysters, shrimp, scallops, fish, and squid filled the air. Hank rubbed his black and white head on my leg. I hadn't realized he had followed. Thank God Ralph didn't. Iris was obviously in shock, so still, multi-colored silk blowing in the breeze. Several firemen and one fire woman manned the huge water hoses, but it was obvious that the wooden structure could not withstand the heat. It crumbled before us. I scratched Hank's ears. He reached over, pawing at Iris.

She jolted out of her stupor, "I'm sorry, too, pup."

Over crabs and beer the evening before, Iris had told me a family legend. Lumpy's Crab Shack was rebuilt a couple of times before. Her great grandfather, Captain Samuel Lumpford, had run a fleet of boats off of Tilghman Island. Fresh rockfish, Maryland blue crabs, and oysters had made "Lumpy's" famous to locals and travelers for many decades.

From what Iris told me, Captain Samuel Lumpford powered out of Knapps Narrows with four men who wanted him to take them fishing. He was just home from World War I and reworked his old wooden boat. While fighting in the war, "Lumpy" dreamed of mornings such as this. The Choptank River gleamed as the red sun rose in the sky. Warm air breezing by, bait in the bucket, home brew surrounding a block of ice. The men had been staying at his parents' inn for the weekend. He had told them about the rockfish he had caught the day before. Art, the oldest, offered to pay him to take them to where they were biting. Lumpy had built the boat as a teenager, motor and all. Worked on automobiles when they came to the island, had learned about powered motors and loved the way he could zoom across the water when sailors barely moved in the still air.

Lumpy's mother, Louise, had packed a big picnic lunch of crab cake sandwiches, sliced cucumbers, and potato salad. He sat it in a large box on top of a block of ice. They brought all the fishing gear he owned, and some chicken necks to catch Maryland blue crabs. An idea formed in his mind as the day wore on. Each fish caught was bigger than the other, and he got a thrill when he pulled in fat crabs on a trot line.

A trot line, I discovered, is a chicken neck tied to the end of a fishing line. You hold it by one end and drop the neck into the water. Watch and wait.

Lumpy helped his dad do repairs at the inn that first spring after the war, but he yearned to be on the water and decided to build another, bigger boat.

By 1930, Lumpy had a fleet of fishing boats and a following built mostly through the inn. Crabbing in the summer was going great. He sold his catch to buyboat operators who then transported the crabs and fish to markets along the shore everyday. He got the chance to buy a small plot of land in St. Michaels, had been thinking of building a crab shack-both wholesale and retail, and that is what he did.

The first fire happened while building the original shack. It sat just across from the Inn at Perry Cabin. These two were opposites. Perry Cabin drew the elite to its upscale four star inn on the Miles River. Top Washington officials often went there for discreet meetings. On occasion the Black Hawk helicopter landed in the side field. And sooner or later, most of those high rollers stepped through Lumpy's wooden screen door. They claim there is no place to get bigger, sweeter crabs. A couple of picnic tables sat out front by the newspaper racks. Inside, you could get home cooked take-out meals. The back counter offered fresh catch everyday. They would steam the crabs for you or sell you the pot and fixings to do it yourself. A little Old Bay Seasoning®, and you were in heaven. Selling sodas, beer, liquor, cigarettes, and lottery tickets kept the place hopping.

Although they had rebuilt three times, the set up was never changed. Never fancied up. Eastern Shore folks loved their ways, were tired of all the changes for the tourists. Visitors enjoyed the culture. The "shack" made them feel a part of the "Land of Pleasant Living" even though they knew they could never really live there. Too laid back. Not enough enterprise. A great place to retire, but to make money in this part of the world year round, extreme ingenuity was required. St. Michaels was quiet over the cool months, but Lumpy's never was. When the western shore wealthy couldn't get to the Eastern Shore of the Bay for their crabs, oysters, and rockfish, they had the fresh catch packed in block ice and transported across the water in fast boats from Lumpy's. Sure, the western shore had crabbers, but they didn't have the mystique and the reputation old Captain Lumpford had built up--that his descendents carried on. Not something easy to match. Quality, consistency, service with a smile.

I wondered who hated Iris so much they would destroy the business her family worked for three generations. The first two times it burnt because fires were caused by careless cooks. Her grandfather and father fired the culprits for their irresponsibility. I knew that was not the case now. She said she checked the place herself at closing time every evening. And that last fire in town was set on the back porch. Paper and gasoline. And now this!

I watched Marley studying the crowd gathered along Talbot Street. I knew whoever set the blaze was more than likely watching, too, enjoying, even possibly putting the fire out. I also began looking at every person's eyes seeking a spark of excitement, joy, pleasure. It got darker as the firelight died. Marley moved closer to the crowd, observing without being too obvious. A young man sat on the curb in front of Perry Cabin smoking a cigarette, cap pulled low, ankles crossed on extended legs. Hank noticed him, too. He sauntered over and gave him one big lick on the face like he knew him already. I followed, sitting next to him while he petted my dog.

"Damn shame," I sighed.

"Yeah."

"You local?"

"Tilghman."

"Staying up here with family?"

"On my way to work."

"Work on a boat?" I had never met a Chesapeake Bay waterman. I had imagined the first one I spoke with would have weathered skin, decades on this kid, and stories to tell.

"Yeah, dredging for oysters today. Sell to Lumpy's, though. Don't know what we'll do with our catch now."

He stood, shrugged his bony shoulders at me, bent at the knees, rubbed Hank's head, then nodded his own capped head. We watched him slide away.

"Hey, what's your name?" I yelled. I had never been a shy person.

"Knapps Reckon. Pleased t' meet you." He nodded again and grinned.

"I'm Cedar Jace. Good luck today."

He smiled, turned, and jogged around the bend to Higgins Marina.

"Lost in thought?" Iris startled me.

"Oh, Iris, how are you holding up?"

"I'll live, but I am not happy."

"I am so sorry. What can I do to help you out with this?"

"I am sure I'll think of something," she sighed.

I put my arm around my new friend's shoulders and we turned to look at the smoking crab shack. She's taller than me, so it was a reach. The air reeked of rotted seafood. Marley ordered the volunteers around.

"I'm glad you're here, Cedar," Iris said in a slow whisper. You have a good heart. I know people. You are my kind. Marley thinks so, too. She is tough, but a softie, too."

"Thanks. That means a lot, but what do we do next?"

"Here comes Sheriff Means. I bet he can answer that for us."

The doughy man shook his head while approaching we pajama-clad gals. "Any ideas?" he asked raising his thick eyebrows, scratching an ample middle.

"Someone is looking for trouble. Found it, too. I want this person nailed to the bulkhead, Eastern Shore style," Iris spewed. Tears flowed down her inflamed cheeks. Anger surrounded her, but her natural grace showed through.

"That's a given. I'll let you know if we come up with any concrete ideas after we discuss the evidence."

"What evidence, Sheriff?" Iris demanded.

"Later," he said, looking at Cedar.

"Oh, Sheriff, meet my new boarders, Cedar Jace and her faithful hound, Hank."

"Good to meet you, Miss." He tipped his hat.

"You, too, Officer."

"Sorry we are not making a great impression as a town. Normally St. Michaels is very low key. Not much crime to speak of. A few unruly canines is all."

"Hank is well behaved," I smiled. "And most times wears a leash."

I stretched, still in my new bed, and watched as the sun rose over the pool in the backyard. I rose and stretched a bit more then went to the kitchen and put the kettle on for tea. The house was quiet, but I wasn't sure if Iris was home or not. Ralph came up alongside me, rubbed his enormous black hairy head against my hip. I had almost forgotten the nightmare that was real. Poor Iris. No wonder I am still tired. I took the tea to my room and began unpacking. Never had the chance last night. Dinner was so much fun. Iris and Marley made me feel like I had been here forever. Friends already! I would miss my life-long friends, but home had grown stagnant for me. Not my friends, but I could no longer find anything to write or get excited about. The strain and grief had me all tapped out. I was terribly drained, bored, and in need of inspiration. Craved it horribly. And now I found it. My mind hummed like a well oiled engine. I opened my laptop, plugged it in, and brought up a blank page. I wrote.

"He watched with laughing eyes as the Sheriff scratched his belly. Flames reached into the night sky heating the air for blocks. He admired the smell of burnt wood. Wanted to grill a steak. He was good at that. Made a great steak, his Mom had always said. And building all those charcoal fires in their grill growing up made him a pro now. He listened as people complained. Watched their sad, angry, determined, lost faces. Sat on his porch, coffee in hand. "Yes, it is awful," he thought. "Iris will need help rebuilding."

CHAPTER 3

I stood amongst the rubble of my new friend's establishment. The fourth fire of this type in as many months, they say. St. Michaels was a thriving tourist village. Now four storefronts were charred shells. Three were in different stages of reconstruction. When I had first driven into town, I had noticed several buildings the construction, but it had not occurred to me that there was a menace among us. I had neither heard or read a thing about it.

The bulldozers would be here to plow to the ground what was left of Lumpy's Crab Shack as soon as the insurance adjuster finished up. It was noon now. I could see Iris walking toward me, head held high, long dress flowing behind her. My landlord loved her dresses and they were very becoming to her long lean figure. I watched as men appreciated her with their eyes.

"Should I even bother to rebuild?" Iris asked me, her face strained.

"What? Yes, of course. Why wouldn't you?"

"I'm tired, and maybe it is time for a change."

"What else would you do?" Not knowing her very well, I was curious.

"I don't know. I've always wanted to travel. This place, as much as I love it, keeps me too busy to see the world."

"Maybe you should take this slow. You can close in the winter and travel if you want. It's always best to take time to think things through, I believe."

"I know," she sighed. "I need to find out who is doing this. Is it someone we know? A tourist? "

"I have no idea, but someone is having a ball at the town's expense. That is evident. Hope they figure it out soon."

"I can't believe no one has been hurt yet. Four fires and no injuries. Thank God!"

"Lucky for them, too."

The insurance adjuster parked his red sedan across the street and walked over to us, pushing his glasses up his nose, clipboard in hand, head shaking. "Iris Jennings?" he asked as he offered his hand. They shook and looked each other over.

"Hi Alex," Marley walked up behind him. She had gotten to know the adjuster from the previous fires. The only thing standing there now was the large walk-in freezer.

"It's the same as the others. Gasoline and newspapers," Marley nodded.

"Well, let me get some questions answered, then I can look around."

"Fine," she mumbled, mind obviously elsewhere while she turned a ruby ring round and round on her finger.

Wispy clouds made for a beautiful sky above. The sun warmed us. God gave us a perfect day weather-wise.

When I returned home, I wrote:

Pouring a glass of milk, he carried his sandwich to the front porch. He loved watching the small town people. A large silky Tabby purred at his feet. Those rose bushes need trimming, he noted. Can't let things get out of hand. The houses in St. Michaels had a standard to uphold. Not like it used to be, when the oyster factories along the harbor kept the town in a constant state of fishy aroma. Those traveling through would roll up their windows and hold their breath, but that was a couple of decades ago.

The town came together. Lots of money people retired here. Improved the houses and shops. Opened Bed & Breakfasts, stores, and restaurants. Made the town a place for retirees to relax in style. Any town meeting would show you who ran things now. Even though many old timers still held ground, it's the newcomers and their money holding the strings of the town today. They rebuilt the library, contributed to the museum, and opened a community center. The Miles River Yacht Club is mostly people from afar. People who have moved here to hide or rest or sail or drink. Some locals still belong, but not many. Hard feelings are a constant undercurrent. Old timers resent the newcomers. Newcomers don't care.

As a teenager I wrote poetry and short stories. When I married I began working at the store and diner and my young handsome husband went off to the service. He couldn't wait to learn to fly helicopters and loved it when he did. I was so very proud of him. So in love with my Rusty. When he crashed into the woods my young heart fell apart. His family had owned the store, and sold it to us at a very low rate for a wedding gift. We were so very much in love. I was devastated when I got the news that he would not return home. Not ever.

I had written and self published several booklets by then, travel guides on the area, mostly. Sold oodles of them in the store. My freelance features on local characters were being read in the Sunday papers and local magazines. It took me some time to write after that blow. I had an infant to raise and threw myself into motherhood and running the business. We lived upstairs and had a mortgage to pay.

Many years later, as I walked along the Youghiogheny riverside one late January day, I felt my destiny. I would write more books, important books. Listening to the music of the white water filled me with love for life and renewed energy. It was three years after Willie's death and I was ready to head to the Chesapeake Bay. Bigger water. Bigger dreams. I had not counted on writing about arson, but I feel I must. I may even solve this mystery. It was I who figured out what happened to my son. The law had no clue who did it or why. I knew in my gut as soon as I saw his lifeless body. There was only one person who resented him. A stranger would not have buried him in the park just up the street from our home, mocking me.

I had always been the best Mom I could be. I gave my son mounds of love and adventure. We took vacations all over the country. It was his laughter that I missed the most. That wonderful full-bodied laughter. We were close, so I knew more than most about what was going on at the middle school. It was not always pretty. I tried to keep on an even keel, but sometimes things happened and I would have to take a stand. Mostly with making teachers do their jobs. They liked to hang outside the building and smoke cigarettes, letting the kids go wild.

It seemed that way now. Someone had to take a stand against this arsonist. My God, they burnt down my new friend's place of business. It's outrageous that someone could get away with four random fires in such a short time in a tiny village such as St. Michaels. Was it a man or a woman? Young, old, in between or a fireman like you hear so much about? They say some enjoy setting fires just to watch them burn. I really did not want to think about that one, but had to admit that flames are very mesmerizing.

I felt in my gut that the fires were a message to the town from someone. What was it they were trying to say? I needed to know. Had the feeling it was the guts of a great story. How could I begin a new life in a town that was burning? I would investigate a bit. It just had to be done.

Where would I begin to seek the information I needed to get to the heart of things? I knew the sheriff may resent my interference, so I needed to be discreet. To watch, listen, and observe. What a great book this was going to make.

"Let's go for a walk, Hank. Get your leash. Come on. Go get it. One of these days you will know that one, right? Humor me," I laughed and scratched his floppy ears.

As we ran my mind reeled. My first day living in St. Michaels was filled with events. Interviewing at the Town Dock, dinner with Iris and Marley, huge Maryland blue crabs no less! The fire. A new novel. My mind tried to sort things out as I walked to the town marina. By now many of the crabbers were finishing with their day. Slips sat temporarily empty. Docks were quiet except for a few pleasure boaters coming in for the weekend. Many had already moved their vessels from the water for the winter. Some construction was happening on the docks at the big blue B&B across the water. I could see so much from the harbor. The Chesapeake Bay Maritime Museum I had read about, the Crab Claw and Town Dock Restaurants and docks, the Inn at Perry Cabin, HUGE houses. I yearned to take a boat ride. People smiled and nodded at me as we stopped running and just strolled along. Hank brought laughter. They were used to Labrador Retrievers and Jack Russells here, not hounds. He loved to run, though, so we took off and ran a few more blocks. We stopped short at the Post Office and went inside to check the mail, knowing it could only be junk. I was right. One flier had specials from Iris' place. It was Friday. I sat on the bench out front to watch and think. In just minutes an older man with a feisty terrier sat beside me. The little guy barked and growled at Hank. Hank woofed at him and sat down staring until he quieted down. He introduced himself as Martin Bakenton, owner of two of the Talbot Street shops. He was worried. Said his shops would go up quickly if set afire. I told him where I was staying and why and he said he needed week end help if I was interested in applying. I said that I appreciated it, and would think it over. He owned a large trading company. Books, clothes, coffee bar. That excited me a bit. He was looking for someone to help manage and market both places. He was getting old. Would soon need a cane. Wanted more time to be old and travel. I said thatI would definitely think it over.

As I walked back "home" I marveled at my luck. Two job opportunities and a book already…in such a tiny retirement village. Smiling to myself, I was not paying attention when I ran smack into the kid I had met on the curb that morning at the fire.

"Knapps, oops, sorry."

"Cedar, right? We meet again," he said, bending slightly from the waist.

"Done work for the day?" I asked noticing his crooked smile.
"Yeah. Had a good day, too."

"I really love this town," I admitted, looking around.

"Have you been to Tilghman yet?"

"No, I haven't."

"Want the tour?"

"Sure. You need a ride home?"

"I could use one. Have a party to go to tonight."

"I'm game. I'd love to see the island. Then you can get to your friends."

"Deal."

"I need to go home and do a few things first. I'll pick you up in front of the Post Office. How's that?" I offered.

"What if I'm a rapist?"

"Then you're dead," I stated, looking him in the eyes. I didn't see a rapist there. I smiled at the kid. "I'll be back in twenty minutes."

"Great. Thanks." He rubbed Hank's ears. It's not like he had a choice. Hank was all over him. Liked him. That meant something. Hank was picky about people. Ignored many, but Knapps seemed to be okay to him. I respected Hank's judgment in humans. He had hated the cook who killed Willie. I will always regret not taking his warnings to heart. How could I know? I really believed Hank didn't like him because he chased him out of the kitchen everyday. He was secretive but I never thought of him as a murderer. Knew he was not especially bright and was a bit arrogant, but he showed up on time and did a good consistent job. I shook those thoughts from my mind. They never left my heart.

We ran home, letting the day sift through my brain. Iris

was not in the house. I left her a note, grabbed a peanut butter sandwich and an apple, and sat on the front porch with a glass of water. The wicker glider was so comfortable. I felt I had been there much longer than a day. So much had happened, but I was not yet tired, although the hammock in the back yard looked mighty inviting. I laughed out loud, spraying apple into the air, as I realized I had just picked up a young fellow. I had a hammer under my Subaru's® front seat at all times and knew how to handle men. I felt there was something about the kid that was worth knowing. He may have information about the fires; he may not. I had to know if he had been there just because he saw the action on his way to work…or another reason. Our unplanned meetings were not coincidence. I was sure of that. Something was leading me to more knowledge. I would find it. Exploring the Eastern Shore. That's me.

Knapps was there waiting with a relieved grin. "I wasn't sure if you'd show."

"Come on. Get in."

Hank jumped into the back seat and licked the kid's face from there before sticking his head out the window. Black ears flapped in the wind. The dog was a happy boy. As we left St. Michaels, I could see water on both sides. He pointed out the Bozman/Neavit Road, Lowes Wharf and Sherwood. I felt great, free for the first time in years. What a beautiful area.

"Do your folks know you're coming?" I asked him.

"Yeah, Mom knows."

"How old are you?"

"Nineteen."

"Did you graduate high school?"

"Yeah, they made me. I didn't like it. Been working on boats since I was little. My dad had a heart attack, died on the water. I was with him-about ten years old. Mom remarried, so I don't like it at home so much anymore."

"Ever think of going to college?"

He paused looking at me and said, "I want to write, but haven't done anything with it. Don't think I'd fit in at college. Don't like sitting and listening to teachers much."

"Knapps, I write, too."

"No shit?" he blurted. "Oh, sorry, but I knew there was something about you that made me feel comfortable. That's cool. What do you write?"

"Whatever I can sell. I've written a lot of local history and travel books, some fiction, lots of articles."

"I wrote a story about my Dad, but no one ever saw it."

"How old were you when you wrote it?"

"About fourteen. My buddies would think I was gay if they knew I wrote."

"Writing is a talent, not a sexual leaning," I punched his

arm lightly.

"You never met Tilghman Islanders. You're in for a treat," he laughed reaching back to rub Hank's flopping ears.

I could see many masts in the blue sky as we approached the Knapps Narrows Draw Bridge that took us over the water to the island.

"They named you after the bridge?" I was a bit taken aback when I saw the sign.

"The water. My Dad loved it. Wanted me to love it. I do. I write about that, too."

"Where is your writing?"

"Mostly on disk. I hide them in my closet."

"Does your Mom know you write?"

"Yeah, she's the only one. I don't let her tell anyone. She hates that. Says I'm good and should show it off."

"I have to read your stuff--that's if you'll let me. But first, show me your island."

"No one should ever come to Tilghman and miss out on Buddy's, so let's go there first. Make a left. Uh, please." he smiled at me while I pointed at a boat. His light curly hair framed his face when he took off the hat.

There was a huge Skipjack sail boat sitting proudly in the front yard of Harrison's Chesapeake House. The old white-washed wooden inn was two floors. Knapps explained that it had been there for many generations in the same family. The rooms were bare-bones. The food, family style.

"The parties get wild here and are known far and wide. On each summer holiday Captain Buddy holds Buns & Wet T shirt contests. Don't mean to offend," he blushed. "There's live music both at the Tiki Bar/deck and inside at two more bars. Huge dining rooms hold a couple hundred people during their weekly all you can eat seafood and oyster buffets. Buddy's is known for great crabs, fried chicken, and hospitality. You'll have fun here."

To the left I saw a shop called "Island Treasures." He said they just built the new shop. It used to be in a trailer. This had a wrap-around covered porch on three sides, with wooden swings and rockers on the porch. I had to go inside and soon. There was a sale rack of "island" clothes on the covered porch. I wanted to rummage through them in the worst way.

We parked in the gravel lot and entered Harrison's Chesapeake House through a huge screened porch lounging area with white wicker furniture and yellow flowered cushions. I could smell fried chicken, but ordered an iced tea to quench my thirst. The captains and their crews were just getting in from fishing trips. Stories bounced around the bar.

"Captain Brevin beat us to the spot again. He must leave at 3am to get out there. We had to watch them pull 'em in for hours while we waited for bites. Soon as we took his place, though, things started happening."

"Ma'am, you can pick up your filets down at the fishing house before the bridge. It's on the right. They'll be ready in about half an hour. May I buy you a beer?"

Men laughed in groups. Families looked sun-burnt and happy. The bar filled and Knapps pulled me by the hand to get going. We then walked out on the huge deck where a tiki bar, dozens of picnic tables, and fishing boats bordered the Choptank River.

I practically drug him into the shop next door, loving the selection of island wear. I made a mental note to return on my own. I would start working on my new look real soon. He had me make a left out of the driveway and go to the end of the island, Black Walnut Point.

"This is where everyone fishes, especially night. You should come in the evening sometime. Great sunsets--at Lowe's Wharf, too. They're known for their sunsets.

"It is so beautiful here," I cooed.

"Yeah, you get used to it, though."

"Would you ever live anywhere else?"

"Don't know yet." He shrugged.

We walked Hank and let him relieve himself while just enjoying the day. "Do I get to meet your Mom?"
"Sure. Her name's Connie. She should be home from work by now. She's a nurse in Easton. Let's go see her before Peter shows up. He's not worth meeting."

We drove to the end of Chicken Neck Point Road. A neat

yellow Cape Cod sat back off the lane, with water views to warm the soul. A green Ford Taurus® was parked in the open garage. We went through the kitchen door where she was busy preparing a salad.

"Mom, I thought you might want to meet someone. Cedar Jace, Mom-Connie. Mom, Cedar. She gave me a ride from St. Michaels. She just moved here. She's a writer. Rents Iris' upstairs. Met her at the fire this morning."

"So nice to meet you, Cedar. How is Iris?" She eyed me.

"Not happy, but she sure is a wonderfully nice lady."

"That is a fact, and she has a good business mind. Did Knapps tell you he writes, too?"

"Mom!"

"Actually, he did, in confidence. I'd love to see his work when he is ready to show it."

"That's enough about me. I have to meet my friends. Cedar, I'll walk you to your car. Thanks so much for the ride and the talk."

"It was nice meeting you, Connie," we both laughed as he hurried me out the door. We could see that he was embarrassed that the only two people who knew he wrote were about to conspire on his behalf.

Connie followed us. "Enjoy the Eastern Shore, Cedar. What a cute dog! Come back when we can chat!"

"Mom!"

CHAPTER 4

Iris was sitting on the front porch with Ralph laying at her feet when I arrived home.

"How are things going?" I asked as I approached, Hank sniffing at Ralph.

Wearily, she sighed, "We really know little yet. At least I don't. I hope they're forming a theory that they can't yet reveal, but I am not so sure they have anything at all concrete."

"I am so sorry this happened to you. Can't imagine what you are feeling."

"I just want this person or persons caught."

"What are they telling you?"

"Not much. All the fires have been set with newspapers and gasoline at the backside of the buildings. That is really all I know in the way of evidence."

"But what do you think? You live here. Know the people. See the travelers. Do you have any ideas or gut feelings of your own?"

Iris looked at her new boarder and smiled. "You have a real keen mind for this kind of thing, don't you?

"I've watched Perry Mason and detective shows all my life. Have spent lots of time writing about interesting cases, have done a bit of P.I. investigative research when Rusty died, and then Willie. I do know that it is often what your subconscious tells you it is, and not what is obvious, whether you're facing it consciously or not."

"May I ask you a question, Cedar? Tell me if I am being too nosy."

"Shoot."

"Why are you single?"

"Wow. That's a doosy. By choice, though. Marriage is something I dreamed of having so many years ago. I lost that dream with Rusty and have been keeping men off the subject ever since."

"Really?"

"Did you love your husband, Iris?"

"Yes, but he was on the water much of the time. It worked well because of that, I think. People tend to smother each other and it seems to kill many romances."

"I noticed. I like to date sometimes if it's worth it."

We both laughed at that.

"But don't you get lonely and scared?" she asked leaning toward me.

"Sure, but not as lonely and scared as I used to. Enough about that, then. Let's go out for dinner, my treat," I offered.

"You're on, my new friend. By the way, what did you do with your afternoon?"

"Met the owner of a couple of the shops. He offered me a job. I also ran smack into that Knapps kid again."

"Really?"

"I gave him a ride to Tilghman and he showed me around the island. Met his mother, too."

"You've been a busy girl. What interests you about Knapps?"

"I guess the way he was sitting there watching the fire. Do you think he knows something?"

"Wow. Not something I considered. It is normal that he would be there at that time. He works waterman hours. Why did you think that?" Iris' face flushed. It looked to me like I stepped on the toes of locals. Everyone knows each other and are protective. Just like home.

"The look in his eyes, I suppose. It was dreamy."

"How so?"

"Maybe he was just sleepy. Teenagers hate getting out of bed at noon, let alone in the middle of the night."

We laughed again and went our separate ways to get dressed. I took a few moments to write…

Reading the newspapers each morning was all he had to do that was constructive in his life. Retirement was such a disappointment. His wife didn't want him in the house all the time, but where was he to go? He took his lanky old self walking in the mornings, looked at the boats coming and going in the harbor. Sail boats, trawlers, cigarette boats, crab boats, skipjacks, tour boats, catamarans. Said hello to others out strolling along, some with their dogs. Bought a cup of rich coffee at Poppi's counter. Talked with the locals. Bored, that's what he was. He didn't care about the state of crabs and oysters. Heard it all too many times. Other people's travel stories held little joy.

Each and every dawn he had three newspapers delivered. That kept him busy and worked his mind a bit. He had been a respected principal at Washington Technical School for thirty years. Now, what? He had few friends. Acquaintances was more accurate. They liked to drink and gamble their retirements away. Seemed to enjoy themselves, too. But he wasn't a drinker. A gambler, either.

As he watched Lumpy's go up in smoke the day before, he sighed, wiped his sweaty palms up and down the sides of his green pant legs. Even the fire didn't thrill him that much, but it did give him some satisfaction. Jealousy for those who were busy with their lives ate at him. He looked at them and didn't know how he could have become something other than productive. Excitement at seeing the town in an uproar was the biggest thing in his life right then. He had always enjoyed fire. Liked the flames, the swirling gray-black smoke, and the mesmerizing effect it brought you. But how could he justify the pain it brought to those ruined, and the joy it brought him? Insurance; they had it; they used it. What's the difference? And those buildings were insured for far above what they were actually worth. St. Michaels was an overpriced tourist trap. Sure, he lived there. His wife had dreamed of living in this smug sailing village since he brought her to its harbor on a chartered sailboat years before. He had promised her. Now he was trapped in a tiny town where nothing much happened. A city man stuck on the Eastern Shore where laid back could not begin to describe the complacency of the people. The service stunk many places you went. Locals really didn't want the tourists or the ones who moved there and called themselves locals. They only wanted their money. Well, they are seeing a time they never thought they'd see. Hell, when they first moved there Martha had wanted to open a fashion design shop. They went to a few local business association meetings. What snobs! It amazed him that these people, who are most often retired and don't need the money they make from the travelers, detest even the travelers themselves. They ARE the travelers. They ALL visited here and fell in love with the place. Now they thought they owned the little town along the Miles River. Martha didn't open her shop. She does consulting work for the rich and advises them on how to dress. Goes to their waterfront mansions. Him, he laughed at the people at the meeting. Told her she would never become someone who had nothing to do but complain about the trash that prosperity brought. Yes, at his first meeting, all they talked about was how awful the town looked at 6am on garbage day.

He raised his hand and said, "No garbage, no money."

He grabbed Martha's hand and walked out. They did not join and never would. Martha advertised her business by word of mouth and the Star Democrat's Sunday paper. After several years of sitting around thinking of how to pass his time, he found a hobby. Watching the fires.

At the Town Dock Restaurant, Iris and I were seated by Amy, one of the dining room managers. She asked me to come in for an interview with her and the other two managers the following day. We sat on the lower level of the deck along the water and ordered a bottle of semi dry red wine. It was deep purple and delicious. We relaxed over mussels smothered in garlic.

"May I ask you a personal question, Iris?"

"Of course, I think!" she smiled and leaned into the table just under the umbrella, thick auburn hair graced white freckled shoulders. A fishing trawler was pulling into a boat slip just below us. An elderly woman in nylon shorts and sunglasses jumped onto the dock and began tying it off.

"How long were you married?"

"Most of my adult life, really. We were childhood friends, then discovered a different love as we grew up. Larry loved me as much as he loved the water. His charter business took us on many cruises, to Europe, and Belize. We had a wonderful life until he got caught in that squall. I sold the charter business after that. The Golden Opportunity fleet still cruises today. The new owners take very good care of his boats."

I sipped my wine and studied my new friend. "How old were you when you married?"

"Nineteen-both of us. He died two years ago. It hurts still, but I am getting used to being on my own…and now I have life in my house again!"

"Hank's pretty lively."

"As are you, my dear." Iris looked at me and laughed out loud.

"What exactly is a squall on the Bay here? I mean, I understand ocean storms and snow squalls, but…"

The waiter came by with our Greek salads heaped high with Feta cheese and smoked salmon.

"It happened suddenly," she said while cutting her salad. "He was alone that morning. Had just gone out to test new sails. The fog masked the approach of a water spout. He had his sails up and it knocked him right down. He was lost in the freezing water. They found him the next day. It was a

43

very cold January morning. The Coast Guard said it blew for eight minutes at seventy four mile per hour. Having your sails up in that gives you no chance. Several other boats also had losses." Tears shone in her sad eyes.

"How horrible!"

"Oh, but we lived well and had a love that is rare in this day. No regrets." The ladies clinked their wine glasses.

"This salad is awesome. What do you know about this place-as a place to work while I build up my writing business, I mean?"

"They are the busiest eatery in town. Good people, and as far as tending bar goes, a great gig. It is a dining crowd. They close by 9 or 10 o'clock. No obnoxious drunks to deal with. You wait on the wait staff and the small bar. Good tips, I would imagine. A few locals frequent the place because it is a nice spot for a quiet after work drink. You may enjoy it. You'll meet interesting people, both locals and tourists."

I pondered that. I wanted to get started. Get some of the local opinions about the fires. Keep my ears and eyes open for leads that may be being overlooked. "Are they busy in the fall?"

"Weekends, yes, very. Sometimes even in the winter, if the weather is mild."

We stopped by the sheriff's office on our walk home because we could see Marley sitting on the edge of his desk through the picture window. The office door was cracked open and we couldn't help but hear the conversation inside.

"What is your theory, then?" Marley asked. "Cause I am coming up empty handed. If it was kids they would have made a mistake by now. Don't you think? This thing is driving me bonkers."

"Yeah, they would've. I really have no tangible clues. Newspaper and gasoline. Everyone has access to them. I let Carl and Jimmy both know that we need names of anyone who fills up a gas can, but they could either go to Easton, work at a pump, work on the docks. Oh, yeah, I told Randy, too. People are still cutting their grass, though. We'll just have to talk to all of them and see what pops up."

"And wait for the next fire?" Marley began pacing, wringing her hands.

"Do you have any better ideas?"

"A reward for information, maybe. The people who have suffered may want to put up some money. Someone has to know something. Don't you think someone must have seen something?"

"You'd think, and that's not a bad idea, Marley. May shake them up, too."

A Harley Davidson® went by and both of them turned their heads, noticing our presence. "It just seems to me that some evidence would show up sometime. Four fires. The town is looking like a freak show instead of a tourist trap," she finished.

"Yeah, 'Fall into St. Michaels' is taking on a whole new meaning," the sheriff agreed.

Marley smirked and took Iris by the arm. We all walked out into the waning daylight. She shoved both hands into the back pockets of her Levi® jeans. People were still coming here. Shopping, moseying around. Media vans could be seen regularly now. Would be nice if they could capture the culprit on film. Oh, my. That is an idea. Maybe I should sit up nights watching and waiting for the troublemaker. Undercover work. SMPD, I thought and laughed out loud, smiling. They all looked at me like I was nuts. I looked each passer-by in the eye as we strolled down Talbot Street. They all seemed normal, innocent, but they couldn't be. An elderly lady waved from her flower bed. A couple of men worked on the town mall roof. Just another lovely evening in the Land of Pleasant Living.

We all headed to Poppi's as the sheriff went back to work. Marley kissed her waiting husband on the cheek and took a seat next to him in the booth. Iced tea with big lemon slices were served. David Landslide was a handsome man. Tall, sandy hair, a big smile. He ran a used car lot and garage on the edge of town. Rented cars and vans to travelers. Marley had said that he loved going to the auctions and buying cheap, selling high. St. Michael's residents didn't mind paying for a nice BMW, Volvo, or Mercedes if it was convenient to purchase. He did well, seemed content with his lot, and adored his ornery wife.

Marley leaned in and whispered, "I have an idea." She smiled at him. Her light cropped hair pushed behind her ears.

"Oh, no!" he laughed. "She always has ideas. It is the Gemini in her."

"I need one of those fancy vans of yours. I want to watch for the arsonist nights, but I want to be comfortable doing it. Try to get him on video."

Weird that she was thinking what I was thinking, I thought.

"Are you a cop now?" Dave asked her.

"Ought a be."

"God help me. Need a deputy?" he offered.

"I love you, Barney Fife." She rubbed his shin under the table with her sneakered foot. "I knew you'd agree."

"It's a great cause, and I'm afraid the lot will be next of we don't patrol. We'll have to be sneaky, though. Whoever is doing this is pretty slick."

"Not slick enough for us, Hon."

Iris and I looked at each other, and them.

"Sounds dangerous," Iris worried.

"Yeah, but what is the other choice? I can't sit still and let some nut destroy St. Michaels," Marley whispered, banging her fist on the table as their meal was served.

CHAPTER 5

I awoke feeling inspired. My interview would go well, I could feel it. Hank licked my face and begged to go for his morning walk. While pulling on my shorts to oblige, he moaned, yipped, was in an all-around rush to get moving. It was very early, still a bit dark. We went out the back way so as not to disturb Iris. She must be exhausted with all that has happened. Hopefully the wine helped her rest and she would have a better day.

We ran the six blocks to the water, passing by the Head Start, a Baptist Church, gift shops displaying very colorful paintings and original art for your home or office, nautical shops bearing ships wheels, lighthouses, chairs shaped like hands, and pink plastic flamingos, and galleries of local photographer's work both black and white and color. Most of the watermen had long since set out for their days oystering, but charter boats were preparing to sail. Dock hands rubbed red eyes. Coffee was being consumed. I could smell the fragrant ground beans. Old men gathered on and around the bench on the town's dock to gab about the latest doings. I knew this was my chance to see what they were thinking about the fires, and, well, men love to talk to girls, so I ventured forth.

"Morning fellas," I smiled. Hank strained to get to them and their blueberry muffins. "Is this the Liar's Bench?"

Two of the men laughed and said in unison, "Yeah, but the biggest liars aren't here yet."

"Is that your first lie of the morning?" I asked as they peered at me like wolves in a pack. Eyes glowing.

That brought several of them toward me laughing and slapping each other's backs. "What's your dog's name?" one asked. "What's your name?" another probed.

"I am Cedar Jace. This is Hank."

"You here for the weekend? You sure are a sight for sore eyes this morning. Sick of looking at these ugly mugs," another said.

"No, I just moved here two days ago. Staying with Iris Jennings. We're from Pennsylvania."

"Welcome to St. Michaels," a couple of them said.

"We can always stand another pretty face around here, especially this early. I'm Gus Wakeford. This is my marina and shop." He stuck out his hand, and this started an array of introductions. I tried to look each one in the eyes and record their names. I was always pretty good at that if I gave myself time to let the name settle in my brain. There must have been seven or eight of them. This would require some memory, I knew, as I enjoyed the men's banter.

"Mind your manners, Gus, and offer the lady a coffee," Al said.

"Thank you, do you have decaf?"

"Old guys always have decaf," Gus smiled. "Milk?" he asked heading back to the boathouse. I could see it had a counter with fishing supplies, a few souvenirs, rates for fuel, boat slips, and bikes and scooter rentals.

"Yes, please."

The sun was already warming their faces, and a mild fog began to lift. They gave me a seat on the bench for which I felt honored. "So, Cedar," Al squinted at me, "What brings you to the Eastern Shore?"

"I hate snow and winter is coming to the Pennsylvania mountains as early as next month."

They nodded knowingly, in unison. A tale they were obviously used to hearing.

"So, what kind of work do you do?" Gus asked.

"I am a writer," I smiled.

"What kind of a writer? Not a reporter, I hope."

"Sometimes, but I write books mostly, things like that."

"What kind of books?"

"Whatever needs written. At home I wrote travel guides and local pictorial history books, published a tourist newspaper and that sort of thing, but my real love is fiction-mysteries are my favorite."

"Ah," they said in harmony, staring at me. I had their undivided attention.

"If you're staying at Iris' house, then you landed yourself into a world of a local mystery," Gus said rubbing his wrinkled chin.

"What is going on with these fires?" I asked, trying on my innocent voice.

"Wish we knew. None of us sleep well and we have been thinking about organizing a watch. See what we can see," Al said.

"That's brave of you."

"We're bored, and we can't just let the town burn down one building at a time." the red haired one said. He stood and began pacing back and forth in front of us as we chatted on the green painted bench.

"Don't think the sheriff has any clues at all. No evidence has been left and there is no time frame to follow." another put in.

"Don't they all happen in the wee hours?" I asked.

"Yeah, that's true enough, but some more wee than others. And on one end of the town, then another. It is gonna take some doin' to catch this culprit." Gus said.

"Any ideas? I have a feeling you guys have a few."

"Ideas, yes; real knowledge, we wish." Al said.

"Anything I can do to help?" I asked.

"Well, you're the writer. We could use a bulletin put out just for this town. Maybe the town should offer an award for information. Write about what the fires are doing to us and try to shake the arsonist out of his tree," Gus said.

"Hmmmm." My mind began ticking on overdrive. Tucking wild strands of hair behind my ears, I listened as I watched this group of friends throw out ideas.

"The shop owners would buy ads in a paper if we had one, I'm sure. They are all grasping at straws with this thing, and the regular media just exploits us. Ruining our town, they are," another said.

"I will sure give it some thought. What should I call it?"

"St. Michaels News," Gus said. "Keep it simple."

"Simple it is. Are you guys here every morning?"

"Where else?" Al laughed.

"See you soon, then, and I'll let you know what I have cooked up. Anyone else own businesses?"

That started a whole lot of answers at one time, "I have two B & Bs," Al said.

"You should stop by our Village Shoppe," another said.

I got up and said my good-byes.

"Great to meet you, Cedar," Gus said. They all nodded in agreement. "You, too, Hank."

The interview had gone well, so the next day I dressed in the tan skirt and white blouse, sneakers and socks that the restaurant management had requested, and readied myself for my first day on the job as a Town Dock bartender. After calling the owner of the shops, and thanking him for the job offer, I decided bar-tending would give me the ready cash and the freedom I needed to get my writing rolling. I did offer help with their marketing, but I could not see myself being a clerk. I'd wonder off looking for something to read!

Thoughts of the *St. Michaels News* filled my head. I had little sleep, tossing and turning, getting up twice to jot down ideas on a legal pad. This morning I ran Hank up the back roads so I wouldn't run into anyone with whom I would have to have a conversation. Thinking was what I needed now. Iris had coffee brewing. How I loved that smell. Felt like home.

"You look like a high school girl in that get-up!" Iris mused.

"Are you making fun of me?"

"Envying your youthful appearance," she said handing me a cup of Joe.

"Envy? With your beauty? Please, Iris, that isn't

possible."

"Well, I AM a woman!"

I laughed and accepted the steaming mug offered to me. "You'll enjoy the Town Dock, I think. They are great guys, and they have a solid business there."

"Well, I better get going. I am letting Hank rest upstairs with the balcony screen door pulled for fresh air. He needs his beauty sleep."

"He'll be fine."

"Will you?"

"Sooner or later, yes." She sighed.

I stopped to check my mail on the way to the "Dock," and went in to meet my new co-workers. Jeff Anderson showed me the computer system which was more complicated than I was used to, but I thought I could wing it until I became a little more confident on that front. His wife, Roey, familiarized me with the bar set-up and the kitchen routine. The bar was in a "u" shape. One side was the service bar for the wait staff. The other side and the end were lined with stools for customers to relax and enjoy a drink or a meal.

The kitchen was huge with over a dozen cooks and prep workers busy singing, whistling, and sweating. Waitresses dipped huge strawberries in chocolate, plopped rounds of butter into bowls, and prepared for the noon rush.

"You can get introduced to all the girls and guys over the

service bar," Roey explained. That's where you are busiest. You serve them first. They will tip you after each of their shifts. Locals at the bar know this is a service bar. There will be times during the dinner rush on weekends when it isn't even possible to serve the people sitting at the bar. There is not room back there for two people to work, so you wait on the wait staff so the diners are happy, and get to the bar folk as soon as you can. It isn't a perfect system, but most of the time it works. One of the managers will ring your checks up for you on weekends and run for some of the red wine that isn't stocked here. That helps a lot. Some of the girls will grab their own beers if they see you are swamped. We are glad to have you here, Cedar," she smiled and shook my hand.

Roey wore a bow tie, and used her hands as she talked. She had been working there for several years, as have many of the 30-odd wait staff. That told me this is a great place to work. Most restaurants find it impossible to keep staff for any amount of time. I was ready to go. Many of the waiters and waitresses made their way over to me and introduced themselves. College kids and full time people my age. Characters, one and all. I could see that.

CHAPTER 6

After work I was wired, so I wrote.

He read the Star Democrat and laughed out loud. No suspects, no evidence. He was proud of his thoroughness, slyness, and his ability to fool the authorities. Seemed to cover most tracks. His wife would be appalled and humiliated had she known. It was imperative that never happened. He would be so very careful. People were scared, angry. God knows some would be watching closely, especially at night. He scratched his chin's two day growth and pondered a moment, stood, pulled his gray sweat pants up and patted his flat belly. Martha would be gone for a few hours. He'd have lunch at Poppi's, listen to the local talk.

He went upstairs, turned on the bath tub faucet, and adjusted the water. Lunchtime is busy in the streets of St. Michaels. Realtors going every which way in their suits and fancy outfits showing waterfront mansions to the rich. Rumsfield and Cheney even bought homes here. The

Eastern Shore has some thinkers, and he was thinking, thinking. It would be quite a trick if he could do this without being detected. He would be so very proud of himself. He had fancied himself a private investigator as a young man. Dreamed he would solve crimes on his own for a living. Gain the respect and admiration of the nation solving mysteries no one else could figure out. This didn't happen, and now he had to have his fun. He could die in the process. The thrill was so very worth it to him. Yes, it was.

I stopped to speak to the sheriff for Iris, but didn't want to interrupt. Sheriff Means paced his inner office with the door ajar. I waited silently in the small reception area as Fire Chief Ramsey ranted.

"It is not one of my fire fighters doing this, Frank. I know the statistics, and I know my crew. They are ALL good, honest, stable people. Hometown Eastern Shore folk. Not one of them has a fire fetish or hates anyone enough to go on a burning spree. Hell, I know this has to stop, but you are looking in the wrong corner." His red face matched his hair, blue eyes blazing. He wheezed as his asthma began to act up.

The sheriff sighed, "I am pretty sure you're right, Randy, but I have to look anywhere I can. Plenty of people buy the daily paper and fill up their gas cans. That's all the real evidence I have! Don't repeat that. My guys are on patrol twenty four hours a day and have seen nothing out of the ordinary. Nothing."

"Maybe that's because this is an ordinary person they are

used to seeing. Maybe one of our residents has lost his or her marbles."

"I know I am losing mine." They turned and walked out of the office together, stood on Talbot Street, arms crossed, looking at the people milling in the streets, going to the bank, checking their mail at the Post Office. "It could be any one of them," the Fire Chief said. "How do we eliminate the innocent and zero in on the culprit?"

"That is the question we need an answer to immediately. I will call a meeting with my officers and see that they pay very close attention to the ordinary in addition to searching for suspicious behavior."

"We must prevent the next fire."

Instead of barging in, I made some ad sales stops at shops, introducing myself and explaining what I was doing.

As I knocked on the third door I came to, I could see smoke spilling from under an inside door in the back area of Justine's Ice Cream Shoppe. I could hear a muffled cry, a woman. I took the four brick steps in a leap and pushed my way through the old wooden door. I pulled my top up over my nose as the cry ceased.

I tried the door knob using my shirt tail but it was locked. More than that, I quickly realized it had been deliberately jammed with a bar from the outside. I removed the bar and rammed the door with my body.

It sprang open with a bang. Smoke billowed and my eyes teared. The place was tiny and I knew that neither of us could last long inhaling the smoke. A dark haired woman clung to a clipboard, as she lay limp on the black and white blocked 1950's linoleum.

I knew there was no time to run for help, so I pulled her to me by wrapping my arms under her shoulders as shelves of ice cream sprinkles and cans of hot fudge fell from the wall. I proceeded to drag her out of the building that way. As soon as I got her outside, I tried to give her CPR to no avail. It seemed like only a minute in my smoke-filled mind before the fire chief ran to us screaming, "Agnes," and gathered the dying lady into his arms, sobbing.

"Agnes!" he wailed. People came running as the man held his dead wife. Fire Chief Ramsey sunk to his knees, crying, heaving, misery consuming his wide frame. The sheriff was at his side on his radio calling in the troops. His childhood friends, always so happy together, now victims in the noonday sun.

They had a murderer on their hands. Black smoke filled the bright blue September sky. The sun shone upon them as Randy cried, holding his wife whom he would never hold again.

Word traveled quickly through the small village. Iris and half the town watched as Marley and her co-workers put the fire out in the tiny ice cream parlor. The pink and white striped awning melted away. It didn't take long to douse the flames. It was a self-contained corner building.

Everyone talked. I could hear their conversations as I lay

60

on the gurney in and out of consciousness, my lungs filled with smoke and char. So much talk. Now I knew from my first night here, that Iris and Agnes grew up together on Tilghman Island. Their husbands had been buddies all their lives, too. They double dated through high school, and all their adult lives. Had memberships to the Miles River Yacht Club and enjoyed the functions there together. Went to all the plays and events at the Avalon Theatre in Easton.

Agnes had been a clown. The funniest woman around this part of the Eastern Shore, they assured me. Laughter filled the air when you were with her. She enjoyed life so much, and was madly in love with her husband. Randy was crushed, everyone agreed.

Marley came out of the wreck of a building and hugged Iris close. Soot and ashes melded into Iris' flowered silk dress, but she held her in a tight embrace.

"He is laughing at us. I can feel it," Marley cried. "She was just taking inventory. She was so excited about opening the first health food shop in St. Michaels."

I looked at everyone standing in the street, raising my head. David Landslide came hurrying down the sidewalk and took Marley's hand in his, shaking his head. "So much for surveillance," he mumbled.

"I just want to smell each of your hands," Iris said flatly but loud enough that the crowd went silent. If you are innocent, you will allow me this. Someone killed my dear sweet friend today. Prove it wasn't you!" she yelled at them. Tears flowed down her cheeks, but she stood firm.

They all knew her and could see she meant business. A line formed in front of her.

There must have been fifty people there. A few walked away in silence. Marley sneered at them. A couple were tourists I think, but the locals were in mourning and conceded, knowing it was a necessary step in finding the killer.

The WBOS van came speeding to a screeching stop along side us just in time to snap a photo for the evening news of Iris smelling the hands of an old local man who lived with his wife behind Justine's Ice Cream Parlour. "Still chewing, I see," she smiled a thin tired smile at him and he nodded his wrinkled head, walked slowly away.

Marley went to the reporter and let her know there would be a statement by the sheriff very soon. She did not want to get them in a tizzy, but they started questioning the crowd. Great headlines this would make, I knew. Iris came up empty-handed in the smell test and sighed with frustration. David offered her a ride.

"Marley is needed here a while, but you look exhausted, Iris. Let me get you home and fix you a cup of tea, huh?"

"Great idea, Hon," Marley kissed his cheek, squeezed Iris' hand. "This lunatic will be found!" she stomped, turned, and went back to her work. A job she was definitely not enjoying lately.

They closed the ambulance doors and I fell to sleep dreaming of the charred Agnes, barely conscious of my burns being tended to, oxygen mask on my face.

I could hear the attendants talking. "We are all so vulnerable," one said.

"This guy needs lynched!" the other agreed. "Someone should be guarding these places all the time. They go up pretty quick with all that old dry wood."

"I bet this arsonist didn't think anyone was in Justine's. They're closed. It was probably a dumb, fatal mistake. Now he will be convicted of murder when caught," the other claimed.

"Everyone keeps saying 'he'," I whispered. "Are we so sure it isn't a woman?"

"Arson is usually a man's crime, but you never know."

"When was the first fire?"

"That's easy to remember," someone answered. "The coffee shop went up in smoke on Memorial Day. They had just moved to the new location over by the library. Bought the place. The insurance guy tried to accuse them of setting the fire to collect the premium, but then all this has happened since. They are building a whole new café. It was an historic building, sad," he sighed. "They used to live by me."

"Yeah, we even thought maybe someone didn't want them there. The brothers who own it are nice and work hard, but people can be weird."

"They sure can," I thought to myself. At the hospital I was treated and released after resting a few hours and passing all my tests. Iris was there waiting for me. The next day I felt physically good enough to go to work. I had no injuries that would be obvious to customers. The few small burns here and there could be hidden, the sorrow and fear in my mind and heart were a bit more difficult to mask, but I knew that in the worst circumstances, pressing on is the best way to keep your sanity. An old man bellied up to the bar and ordered a malted scotch on the rocks. "Lunch of champions," he laughed. "I'm Doc, who are you pretty lady?

"He's harmless," Chef Sammy smiled at me from the service area.

"Cedar Jace," I said putting the drink on a fresh cocktail napkin.

"You new in town? I know everyone, so, of course you are. You're the girl who tried to save Agnes. How are you feeling today?"

"Better, thanks. Yes, I'm a writer from Pennsylvania. Staying at Iris Jennings's place."

"Lucky you. I'd like to stay there myself."

We both laughed at that and I asked him, "Have any theories about the local arsonist?"

"Yeah, I think it's a bored old man toying with us and laughing his ass off."

"Why do you say that?"

"There are a lot of bored old men around here."

"Are you bored?"

"Not at the moment," he grinned looking me up and down as I walked to the service bar to make a few drinks for James and Jan and to mull over the Dr.'s theory.

When I refilled his scotch, I asked, trying my best to be nonchalant, "Why do you say it is an old man setting all these fires? Maybe it's a bored crazy woman."

"You got me there. It's just my gut reaction. I am 78 years old. I work full time, lecture, work out, enjoy my family. My life is very full. A lot of the men my age around this village find it difficult to fill their time productively. Idle minds and all that. Think of the many wasted brains around here. Retired Union Leaders, CEO's of this and that, former professors, retired principals, politicians, realtors, what have you. Now they live in a place where there is little to use up their time. They are not watermen, so they don't hang out with those guys. Some of these retirees go to the yacht club and drink a lot of days away. I would say it isn't any of them. They're pretty harmless," he laughed deep in his belly.

"How do you know they are ALL harmless?" I asked him.

"They're old and they're drunk a lot. Nice men, don't get me wrong. Professionals, but not criminal or bitter. They have routines for the most part, and pride."

"So, if you had to guess, you'd say the arsonist has no pride?"

"You are a curious one aren't you?"

"I am a writer and am starting a newspaper here; also writing a book, so yes, I am curious, and have personal reasons for wanting this stopped."

"God, don't quote me!" The doctor's face turned a bright shade of pink as he spit his drink out in faked shock.

"I won't. You are just speculating here. You are interesting and have given me a line of thought that had not occurred. I was thinking it was a disgruntled shop owner or someone who wanted to open a shop, but for some reason couldn't. Someone bitter."

"Oh, they're bitter and disgruntled alright. It could well be someone younger, or even a female, but my money is on a cantankerous old fart. A sly one, not sly enough, though. Now this someone has committed murder. Got too excited about winning the game. Now they must be scared. Was laughing at all of us until this. Bet he…or she, is sweating and shaking and maybe even crying in their wrinkled old hands."

"You are a kind soul, aren't you?"

He laughed some more. Almost choked. Todd came up behind him and clapped him on the back. "Don't die here, Doc. Bad for business."

"Hey, Todd, I like your new gal. She has a head on her shoulders."

Todd just looked at each of us. I went about my work,

thinking, thinking. It would soon be time to end my shift. I needed to get home; see how Iris was doing. Walk Hank and get out into the world. So much to do. God knows when this lunatic would strike again, and I meant to nail him when he did. He could have killed me.

As I drove through the back streets I watched each person I saw walking, biking, scootering along. Watched them each closely. Went to the Post Office. Looked each person I came into contact with in the eyes. I saw a lot of worry, fear, sadness, and anger, but no guilt.

CHAPTER 7

When I stopped by I could see through the window in the oak door as Fire Chief Randy Ramsey paced the living room he had shared with his wife for over twenty years, tears streaming down red cheeks. A man who looked just like him sat at the kitchen table staring out the window. I felt odd listening in but couldn't help myself.

"How do I live without her?" Randy was mumbling. "I don't know how to go about life by myself. She was my world, my partner, my love. I have nothing here now. This is just a house without Agnes, Rod, it's not a home. Just a house." He stood there slouching, arms hanging low against his muscular thighs. Old gray sweat pants and shirt covering him.

"I could move in with you and then you'd wish you were alone!" his brother tried to humor him.

"Yeah, that's probably true." He almost smiled through

the whisper. "You always were a slob and a pain."

"Now that's the spirit."

"I don't know when it's going to sink in, but this is not something I ever thought would happen to me. I thought she would outlive me by at least twenty years."

"We all did."

"Thanks!"

"Well, putting out fires is a bit dangerous."

"I found that out the hard way. Dangerous when you don't get there in time."

They sat in silence drinking from coffee mugs. The table was heaped with casseroles and baked goods. Comfort food does not always do the job it is meant to do. Rod poured dark rum in his coffee. Passed the bottle to his brother.

They had been there together for many hours, since Rod picked Randy up at the hospital. Randy was grieving and was surely angry enough to kill the murderer. I know how that feels.

"So, how do we find out who is doing this? Who killed Agnes? I have to know!" his face was dark with anger, glossy with sweat.

"Randy, they'll lock you up if you go after this guy."

"That doesn't matter. Agnes is dead. I want to be dead, too."

Rod looked at his brother and grabbed his wrist. "I can't have you dead or in jail. I need you alive. Who the hell will keep me straight?"

Randy looked at him with a blank stare. "Do I look like I can keep anyone straight?"

"You'll gain strength over time. You'll heal some. You'll miss her all your life, but you can survive this, Randy. You have to."

"No I don't."

"I'm staying with you to see that you do."

"Then we have to formulate a plan to get this guy. Any ideas?"

"Yeah, let's get some rest and sober up. Won't get him like this. We are both exhausted and this booze isn't helping any."

"It numbs me so I can't feel," the fire chief mumbled.

Rod wrapped an arm around his brother's waist and led him to the sofa. Covered him up with a maroon afghan. He laid down on the opposite sofa. I couldn't bear to knock on the door until they had some serious shuteye. Randy was snoring before his head hit the pillow. Rod turned the coffee mug in his hands and looked out the window. I nodded at him when he caught my eyes. Old men and women walked their dogs. Couples held hands and shopped. Kids went by on skate boards, while his brother's life fell apart. I walked away.

Agnes haunted me--her scream, her stare, already gone from this world when I found her. Smoke is a quick killer and she had no chance locked in that tiny storage room. I told the sheriff when he came to the hospital about the locked door. It had been secured from the outside. Someone killed her purposely and they knew I knew and that the law now knew. This was no arsonist just looking for thrills. Everyone seems to have loved Agnes, so why murder her? In small towns, I know, the surface did not always reveal the truth. Who hated this lady?

Martha had her bridge game every Monday at 2pm. They met at the Miles River Yacht Club, had appetizers and drinks, talked and played. The foursome was made up of an elderly seamstress, Martha, Maria, and the Commodore's wife. For the most part this particular Monday was no different. Everyone was on time. The kitchen staff prepared an array of snacks for their pleasure, and the bartender was in place. But the conversation and tension in the air was very different. They all knew Agnes and Randy. All liked them, felt vulnerable and were afraid. The seamstress was 87 years old. Her name was Gerti Forbes. She led the ladies, mainly. They adored and respected her. She still worked full time, and did a great job mending and tailoring.

"We all feel bad today, don't we?" she began. "I was with my sister when she made the sale of Justine's to Agnes. They didn't want anyone to know about it until everything was signed and finalized. Agnes was thrilled to

*be going into business and planned some significant
changes. No one could have foreseen this."*

*Martha spoke up. "I was shopping in Easton when it
happened. When I got home everything looked normal in
town except for the burnt building. Still smoking a little,
but not burnt to the ground like some of the others. What
sort of animal are we dealing with here?"*

*"A man, I believe," Gerti smirked. "No woman could do
this, don't you agree?"*

*They all shook their heads in agreement as their drink
orders arrived. Always the same for each one of them. A
round of white wine to start, glasses of water, a toast.*

*Maria, who owned the Christmas Shoppe with her
husband, spoke up, "To Agnes and Randy. May she rest in
peace. May he find a way to build a new life without her."*

"Amen." They raised their glasses in unison.

*Meanwhile, Martha's husband sat on the back porch,
biting his craggily fingernails. His nerves had wracked him
since the death. He took to wearing sunglasses to hide his
worried eyes. Told people his cataracts were acting up.
They were, but he felt he could not afford for anyone to see
his fear. He feared they could smell it. He could. It was
thick in the air. That fire could have spread to their home.
Damn, why did this have to happen? Main Street wasn't so
pretty anymore. The cuteness of the town always irked him.
Martha loved it, though. It was a big part of why she
insisted they move there. She was very happy, finally. She
had hated the D. C. area. So rough. So fast. She was a new*

woman here. Smiling from sun up to sun down. Not him. He was bored. That boredom led to this relentless sitting and thinking. He thought of hobbies he may take up besides his

gardening to replace the thrill he had gained from watching the fires. He knew he could not afford to continue, but could he stop himself now that he so looked forward to them? Could he take up chess, fishing? He wasn't sure.

I checked my mail and as I bent at the knees to reach into my mail box, I noticed an old man checking his mail next to me. One of his pant cuffs looked like it had a soot stain along the rim. I knew soot when I saw it. I used to have a coal furnace. His outfit was deep green, like a mechanics' uniform. It barely showed, but I followed him none-the-less.

I knocked on the wooden part of his door, stood there taking in the colorful flower bed. Brilliant reds, purples, yellows. I could hear someone shuffling slowly across what sounded like a hardwood or tile floor.

"May I help you, young lady?" He grunted through the royal blue screen door.

"Yes, I saw the sign out front about antiques. Is that your business?"

"My wife does that sort of thing. Why do you ask? Got a mansion to redecorate?" he smiled, showing noticeably false teeth.

"Is she in?" I asked. "I'd like to help her promote her business."

"Really, now? Well, she's not here at the moment."

"Maybe you could give her this information for me," I suggested, waving it into the air. I will call on her later. I am starting a local publication which she may want to be involved with."

"I can give it to her," he said, opening the door just wide enough to accept the brochure into his arthritically curled hand.

"You new around here? Haven't seen you before today."

"Pretty new, yeah. I have been in the publishing business for over twenty years, though. I come from a white water rafting village in Pennsylvania that is similar in many ways, to St. Michaels, except for the fires." I kept his eyes locked with mine. "They are pretty scary," I finished.

"Fires usually are," he hadn't flinched. "You expect some mention of them. It's all anyone talks about anymore." He didn't look at me any longer. Blinked. Looked away.

I noticed his fingernails were chewed down. A few had been bleeding recently by the looks of them. Stressed about something. "What is your wife's name? Does she have a card?"

"She'll call you if she is interested," he remarked, looking at me intently while closing the door in my face.

I canvassed a few more businesses who were worried,

scared, and very interested in having a voice for the town. Then I walked back to the docks to see if any of the fellows were at the bench this time of day. Gus was there reading the newspaper. He had several of them piled on the dock at his feet, and looked up as I approached. "Hello there pretty lady."

"Hi Gus. How are you today?"

"Old and cantankerous mostly, but better now that you're here. Sit. You must be sore and weary."

"Yeah, but I worked up a brochure of advertising rates for the *St. Michaels Press*. Just started passing them out to the shops and restaurants."

"You don't waste any time, do you?" he grinned.

I smiled back and took a seat where he patted the bench. "Where's that handsome dog of yours?"

"I'm going to walk him later. I had worked at the Town Dock today. I'm sure he is wondering where I am."

"Things have been pretty wild around here since you moved in. Still like St. Michaels?"

"Yeah, but I feel sorry for everyone. How awful. Any ideas who could be doing it? A murderer now whoever it is," I claimed, fishing.

"Yeah, I bet they hadn't expected that. Most arsonists just like the thrill of the flames, the power. Now he'll be hunted down like a dog and God help him when he's caught. This is the Eastern Shore. If someone besides the law catches on to him, I wouldn't want to be him."

"It's called 'Mountain Justice' where I come from."

"Same thing, I'd imagine. But how are you settling in? How's Iris?"

"I'm settling, but I must get home to see how she is doing. She has had a rough time."

"What a brave woman she is."

"Yeah."

"So, are you really going to put together a newspaper for this little village?" Al asked as he approached them and took a seat on the bench.

"I believe so. Many things are going through my mind. Columns, features, etc. There is plenty to write about."

"I can't wait to see what you have to say," he smiled. "Have you read the Washington Post today? People will be coming here in droves just to take pictures. Great time for you to get started. Extra, extra, read all about it!"

I got up and sighed. "I better get to it, then. Good talking to you guys. See you soon, and thanks for the initial idea!"

"Good luck, little lady. Get some rest," Gus said.

CHAPTER 8

I knew that it must be Iris' brother when I saw him. Erich McKnight parked an old blue Volvo® station wagon behind the Acme and walked down Talbot Street. My heart leapt at the sight of the tall dark haired, broad shouldered man. He wore chinos, a chambray shirt, and deck shoes. Watching that walk of his sent electricity up my spine. I just stood and gawked at him as if I'd never seen a handsome man before. But it wasn't just that. The air had changed when he stood next to the car and pushed his hand through his hair.

When I asked Iris about a picture she had of him, she said he had left years ago to make it big in Baltimore as a Private Investigator, and lately, cheating husbands and wives were starting to bore him. It was always the same old thing. Someone was stepping out-usually both were when all was said and done-and nothing good came from his work. On occasion he had solved a tough mystery. A couple murders, a missing person or two, and he had built a reputation as a stand-up guy. Even had friends on the city force, but a few enemies, too.

Erich and Iris grew up on Tilghman Island. He went to Washington College in Chestertown and then lived in Easton for a few years. Started his practice there before heading to the city. Missed the Eastern Shore and talked of moving back, but wasn't sure there would be enough work to support him, enough excitement to keep him humming. When he called I answered the phone. He'd said he missed his sister, was worried about her, and planned to come to Agnes' funeral. He had not heard that Iris' place got torched and Agnes died until her small voice on his answering machine scared him into tossing a bag into the car.

He went to Poppi's. It was high noon. The place was filling up. It was a superb September day. One for the books weather-wise. Crisp air, shockingly blue skies, 75 degrees. But this arsonist seemed to be striving to reduce the town to ashes and sadness, and was succeeding by the looks of folks and Talbot Street. Anger is what was in the air. No one who lived here all their life would do this, right? I felt sick in my gut. A blonde, smiling waitress approached him as I entered and he ordered a club sandwich and iced tea, unsweetened. "Hold the fries," he told her. "Gotta watch my figure."

"I'll watch it for you," she promised, made eyes at him, and went about her work.

I had left Iris a note saying exactly when he would get into town. He had said that he called their mother would go there later today. She ran a small deli on the island. Catered parties. She was a hard worker and a looker, Iris said. Since their dad died a couple years ago, she hadn't dated at all. Everyone wondered if she ever would. Seemed happy alone. She was like that, Iris said. Enjoyed her own company better than most people's. Funny, smart, had a good life. Traveled in the winters visiting friends around the country. A lot of them were people who came to the island each year. She could have a long distance lover, I thought, but didn't say. They'd never know. While he ate his sandwich, he nodded at familiar faces until a smack on his back made him choke.

"Sorry, Erich," Marley said patting the spot between his strong shoulders some more to relieve the bread in his throat. "Great to see you. We have missed your handsome face around here."

"Marley, you rascal." he grabbed her in a bear hug then held her at arms length. "You look like a million bucks. Married life is good to you."

"I like it," she giggled. "Next to my husband, you must be the best looking man in Maryland!"

They had obviously known each other all their lives and had a tight relationship. He threw a few bucks on the counter and went to a booth with her. Dave soon joined them and when I came back from the restroom, so did I.

"God, the town looks sorrowful," he began. "This isn't right. Can't go on."

"You got that right," Dave said. "Any ideas on how to stop this lunatic?"

"Nothing I'd care to discuss in public. Give me a day or two. Right now I am here for the funeral…and the beer."

"Good, but no one will believe that." Marley said. "Hey, Cedar, join us," she called when she saw me.

My breath caught in my throat when he stood up to greet me. "Erich McKnight at your service," he bowed. I swear lightening struck. We stared at each other like idiots. Kept our hands clasped far longer than a normal shake.

"OK you two. There are other people in the room," Marley snickered. "Sit down and behave." We both blushed, but kept our eyes on each other. Mesmerized like fire. The waitress approached and broke the spell.

"What can I get you folks today?"

"Three specials and iced teas," Marley said. "That OK with you, Cedar?"

"Yeah, sounds fine," I mumbled.

Dave spoke up and told me that Marley had grown up with Erich and that Iris was his half-sister. I could see the resemblance immediately in the high cheek bones, and wide smile. There was a look in his eyes that rang familiar. He wore no ring. For some reason that suddenly mattered to me.

"We spoke on the phone," was all I could muster. I sat my bag on the floor and out fell a brochure. Erich picked it up. Handed it to me.

"What's up?" Marley peaked her eyebrows.

"I am starting a local paper. These are advertising rates. I've been visiting businesses."

"You waste no time. I'm impressed. Cedar just moved here from Pennsylvania. She rented Iris' top floor. She's written a pile of books and has had newspapers and magazines before," Marley told him.

"What sort of paper?" Erich inquired with a curious smile which made little creases form on the sides of his deep brown eyes.

"Local news, events, quirky stuff the daily papers don't publish or have no way of finding out. *The St. Michaels Press*. A rag all our own."

"Count me in," Dave said. "That's a great idea. Is it a weekly?"

"If I can get enough interest."

"When do you plan on the first issue coming out?"

"In two weeks if all goes well."

Marley laughed. "We sure have enough going on around here. Maybe you can put out a special bulletin warning the arsonist we are not as friendly a town as he might think!"

Our lunch arrived. Fried oyster salads and French fries. I had a hard time concentrating on my food sitting across from Erich. The chemistry was thick in the air. When we finished, I excused myself saying that I had to get home.

"Let me walk you if you don't mind. I need to see Iris,"

Erich offered "See you two later," he waved.

"Now that's a handsome pair," I heard Marley observe.

"My wife, the matchmaker." Dave took her hand and led her out the door. I felt them watching us in animated conversation walking up Railroad Avenue.

" The writer and the P. I. Now this is getting interesting," I thought, smiling up at him because, hell, the knot in my throat wouldn't let me speak much.

When we saw the sheriff in the distance, Erich called to him and told me that his long time friend loved his job. For years he had jumped up every morning eager to walk the streets of his clean little crime-free town and nod at the dog walkers, joggers, early risers. Lately, though, things had changed. Normally the toughest problems he had were small drug users being too casual on the corner next to the old oyster house, weekend warriors, D.U.I.'s, and an occasional fight in a tavern. Nothing dramatic. Warnings were given to most. An arrest was rare. He had graduated top of his class, but never considered himself able to be the kind of cop you see on *Law and Order*. He was no investigator, no detective. The stress of that kind of police work was beyond his capabilities. He was not a tough guy. More an "Andy Griffith" type fellow watching over his quiet "Mayberry;" minus the "Barney Fife."

The arsons intrigued him, scared him, gave him nightmares. He knew how to look for basic evidence when there was some. This guy hadn't been leaving any. Wore gloves, probably a hat, too. No witnesses. No DNA. So, how did he find this culprit? He was being pressed hard. Agnes is gone. Randy is at his wits end. Many, he knew, were about to form a lynch mob of sorts. Eastern Shore folks were proud and would not put up with being intimidated and treated like fools.

A slap on the back of his head knocked his hat to the ground. "Frank, you dog," Erich had him in a bear hug before he knew what was happening.

"McKnight! Am I ever happy to see you."

"I'll bet." he nodded, pursed his lips. "Who the hell is torturing this town, Sheriff?"

"If I knew he'd be locked up tight, wouldn't he?"

"Any leads?"

"None I can discuss with civilians."

"You have no idea, do you? Someone threw a hard fast ball into your quiet little world, and you don't know which way to turn," he accused.

The sheriff looked at his shoes. Erich knew him. There was no reason to try to fool him. He could read his face, mannerisms, was no fool. "If you need some assistance, I am here for you. No pressure. I'd love to see this guy stopped immediately, and Iris needs to settle this thing."

"How is she?

"Hanging by a thread. I'm glad she has company."

"Yeah, I could use a set of professional eyes and ears around here. Someone objective. Everyone is so emotional now. I'm afraid if they get the idea it is someone in particular, they'll kill him before knowing for sure."

"Yeah, he could end up in the Miles River in no time."

"You see what I mean. I am at a bit of a loss, I admit. And now Randy is so deep in grief he is no help to me."

"I thought you'd need me. This is no shoplifter. I have dealt with plenty of wackos in the city. Let's put our heads together and see if we can't stop this freak."

"Amen."

At Iris', the siblings hugged. She cried and told him the details of her fire and of Agnes losing her life. He probed her to go on. I took the dogs out to the pool so they could have some privacy and yes, so that he could get a load of me in my swim suit—doing laps.

"But what did you think of him?" she asked me after Erich left to go to Tilghman. "It looked to me like you two were hitting it off," Iris took a sip of her red wine.

"He's very nice," I said.

"He's very nice," Iris mocked. "Please, I know chemistry when I feel it, see it. Christ there were sparks flying hot enough to start another fire! Oh, God, I didn't mean that, but you KNOW what I do mean!"

"It was a bit warm, frothy," I smiled big enough to crack my face in half.

We had a light dinner on the front porch, enjoying the evening, the dogs, the break. A few young children rode their bikes up and down Railroad Avenue stopping to ask if they could pet Ralph and Hank. The mutts (don't tell them I called them that!) agreed to let them.

"He is a good man, you know. Always was a fun guy. Fun kid. Liked to solve mysteries even then. When my bike got stolen on the island, I was ten. He found it in McDaniel in some kid's garage. I was stunned. He had ridden all over peeking into sheds, garages, around the backs of houses until he found it. Made that urchin apologize. He was no older than us, but he's in jail for beating his girlfriend nowadays. Started young, I guess."

"Mmmmm."

"That's all you have to say. A gorgeous, smart, exciting guy drops in your lap and mmmm is the best you can do?"

I laughed into my wine, causing it to go up my nose. I coughed, choked, laughed some more. The neighbor kids looked at us like we were crazy. Our salads were almost untouched. When we calmed down, I got serious. "Do you think it could be an old man setting the fires?"

"An old man? I imagined a young man for some reason, why?"

"No real reason. There are just so many around."

"Can't argue with that logic. Can't imagine why an old man would be so mean. Oh, God, many of them are, aren't they?"

"So are old women. And young!"

They laughed at that. "How is your newspaper coming?"

"Well, it won't come along at all if I don't get to work on it. I did get some good response from the shop owners today, though. They are desperate to get the word out about their sales to the locals since things are in such a state now."

"Don't blame them. Strike while the iron is hot. I'll advertise when I know when I can get back open again."

"I'll count on it."

I headed up to my suite, turned the computer on, and began building the masthead of the newspaper. The first headline read, "Who's Afraid of the Arsonist?" I had decided to put out a four page sample paper and distribute it around town in the next few days to stir things up. See if anyone got upset after seeing what I had to say from a newcomer's view.

CHAPTER 9

Randy had insisted that the casket be closed. He didn't
want everyone gawking at his wife. He did not want to look
at her dead, either. He was tired of the sympathetic
offerings, he'd told Marley. He wanted answers, not pity.
He wanted a reason for this loss. He wanted Agnes back.
But there she was, in a wooden box about to be lowered
into the ground forever. He hated that, but that was her
wish. She did not believe in being turned to ashes and put
into an urn. She felt she should turn to ashes in her own
good time. But the arsonist had come close to handling that
for her, hadn't he? Was he here? Randy, Rod, Marley,
Dave, Iris, myself, the sheriff and his deputies scanned the
crowd. We all felt we should be able to see it in someone
we knew or were acquainted with, even a stranger. How
could a friend or acquaintance be that great of an actress as
to fool everyone for so long a time? These were bright
people. Not fools.

Erich stayed in town, ball cap pulled down over his eyes

last I saw him. The streets were virtually deserted except for a few old timers checking their mail. A gorgeous blue sky gave one the feeling that all was right with the world, but it surely wasn't. He went into the Post Office and stood behind a lady he did not recognize. The Postman addressed her as "Martha." She seemed sweet, harmless. He nodded a good morning greeting to her and opened the door when she began to exit the room into the area where all the mailboxes stood waiting-stuffed with bills and circulars. An old man met her at the door. He was buying the morning papers. Several of them. He watched as they entered the Acme. There were many such retired couples on the Eastern Shore these days. They came from Philly, D.C. and New York for the moderate climate. And they drove real estate prices through the roof vying for the framed houses, making Bed and Breakfasts of them. Who would want to share their home with strangers, changing dirty sheets, cleaning commodes during their golden years? An odd concept in my mind.

An old man sat on the bench just outside the Post Office with his black curly haired dog. Erich joined him. "Fine day for a funeral," he commented.

"There is no good day for a burial," the old man snarled.

"I guess you're right about that. No good day," Erich agreed.

He smelled smoke. It was coming from the Video Store/Flower Shoppe. He could see it as he ran, yelling for the man to call 911. They always strike during gatherings when they think no one is watching, he thought, running up the sidewalk. In a moment, sirens rang in his ears. Randy and Marley were the first ones on the scene. Agnes would want it that way, they all knew. Erich picked up a dollop of tobacco that lay on the back stoop. A tiny dropping. Maybe he smoked a pipe, rubbed. Evidence, maybe, at last.

I delivered my first sample of The *St. Michael's Press* the day after the video store burnt. I printed only a few hundred copies on my own printer in a booklet style, letting people know the next one would have more stories, photographs and ads, newspaper style. I had written this introductory issue from the heart, no advertisements, just the view from a newcomer about what was happening to St. Michaels and its residents, its historical buildings, its image. I had never seen the town before, so I had nothing to compare it to, but knew what I felt. Could see what the arsons and the murder were doing to the people around me.

Beware! Arsonist, Murderer was my headline. I prayed they wouldn't come after me at Iris' house, but Iris encouraged me to make a stand. Helped me fold the publications, and deliver them. She seemed to need to take some action. Her insurance check was on the way, but she said she wanted revenge, to scare the bastard, to catch him and toss him in the Miles River, run over him with an active propeller.

Residents, too, were thrilled something was being done. They took the papers and stacked them on their counters. Poppi's, the Post Office, you could find them all over town. They even allowed us to put them in the visitor center. Iris was a sponsrr. She told them she was backing the publication. Well, she would be an advertiser soon enough, she rationalized.

The article stunned people. They were sick of the big papers depicting them as a sideshow. They came up to me and shook my hand. I had put into words their anger, fear, and feelings of revenge in a way they could not have done. By taking action on their behalf, I had made many friends, and very possibly, a dangerous enemy. This would be a successful endeavor by next summer, I knew, but I did it because I couldn't sit by and watch the arsonist win. And he sure seemed to be winning.

At lunchtime we ladies plopped ourselves into a booth at Poppi's and breathed a sigh of relief. We had done our part. Everyone kept coming over to us, paper in hand, thanking us for our efforts.

"This should scare him out. Make him shake in his boots," Poppi's proprietor, Jane Manning said. "Eat up girls, it's on the house today," she smiled as she set the lunch specials and iced teas before us."

"Wow," Iris exclaimed. "This is a first!"

"Good deeds and all that," Erich said as he slid in next to me.

I all but jumped. The thrill that seared through me when our thighs touched ran a jolt through me like I had never before experienced. What the hell was going on? I tried not to let it show, but didn't know how it couldn't. Was he feeling this?

"Hi, Erich," Iris smirked at her brother. "Any luck yet?"

"Maybe. I can't say. No, don't get excited," he told us because we both dropped our forks and leaned toward him hoping for great news.

"We're not exactly hot on the trail, but I hope we at least have the beginnings of the trail. A small thing to go on."

"Well, give it up!" Iris grabbed his wrist. "This bastard is ruining our lives!"

"Easy, Sis," he soothed. "I can't leak this. I have to follow the lead without people yapping about it, writing about it. He'll know we're on to him…or her."

"Which is it?" Iris insisted.

"I hope we know soon, but I don't see a woman doing this. My gut tells me that."

"Mine, too," I mumbled.

Martha felt worried that her husband showed signs of debilitation. He never took to retirement the way she had; the way many folks in the little town had. He was a loner most of his life. Didn't form friendly relationships with men. She had wanted to join the yacht club. He thought that was silly. They had no boat. She argued that they didn't need a boat. They needed friends. He said he saw no reason for that. When you had friends they always wanted to come to your house. He didn't like visitors. They also liked to invite you over. He didn't want to go to strangers homes.

He read his newspapers, went to the Post Office, cut the grass, weeded the small gardens, but not much else. He was an intelligent man. Ran an entire technical school for engineers. Was used to being surrounded by bright minds. She wondered what went on in his. She loved playing bridge with the ladies from the auxiliary. She loved the little town, and making friends, and knew it was all at the expense of her husband's happiness.

What was she to do, though? Move? Where? Back to the D.C. area? She couldn't bear it. Wouldn't think of it. He never complained. He just didn't LIVE. Was surviving. Trudging through. Thank God he was not a drinker, she mused. She wanted to push him toward a hobby, but what would that be?

"I am going to call that girl with the new newspaper," she told him over breakfast. "Did she seem nice? Everyone is talking about her paper."

"Humph!"

"You met her. What did you think?"
"Seemed nosy to me."

"Reporters are curious people. Her article about the fires was amazing."

"Really? In what way?"

"The insights a newcomer can have are objective and she hit the nail on the head. She posed some hard questions for us all."

"I guess."

"You don't seem to care about anything anymore," she accused gently, her face red with frustration.

"I care about you."

"Do you?"

"Of course. You and only you."

"Is that enough to keep you happy?"
"It better be. There's really nothing else to do here but look at your wife!"

"You could join the club."

"I don't care about that and would never spend the money we have coming in so foolishly."

"Enjoying life is never foolish unless you are hurting someone."

He looked at her over the *Washington Post*. "I enjoy life just fine."

"Do you?"

"Martha, I am an old man. Old men don't need to prove they're interesting anymore. We just need to keep our health and find something to smile about sometimes." He smiled at her.

"What are you smiling about now, dear?"

"Maybe I'll work on an ad for your business today. Take

it over to that reporter for her next edition."

"That would be nice," she felt better. He had something to occupy him at least for the day. She began to take the newspapers he had read to the recycle bin. He stopped her, saying he wanted to go through them one more time. Look over similar advertisements. She had been noticing that they never had to have the newspaper bin emptied by the recyclers, and wondered why. Though he might be using them for mulch again. She had asked him not to do that, but he did like doing the work in the flower and vegetable gardens. She hated dirt and weeds.

CHAPTER 10

Mid September found the Eastern Shore basking in 75 degree weather that brought travelers in abundance on the weekends. It was a different crowd than the summer tourists. These people shopped, left the kids behind. Restaurants were busy. Waitresses and bartenders made more money.

I was enjoying my part time job at the Town Dock. My co workers were local characters. Many of them had been there for years. I felt at home, comfortable. It surprised me that I already felt that way in a new place. Being lonely was a private fear I had suppressed about the move, but I had no time for that. Already I had good friends, profitable work, a newspaper, and was building a reputation as a writer. Erich gave me something to look forward to-that thrill. Although we had not been on a date with all that was happening, and I did not think I could "date" at this time, just knowing he was around town made me smile.

There were a few characters who popped in at the Town Dock bar for a couple drinks at certain times on a regular basis. It was not a place where people went to party, but to relax, to enter into interesting conversations, and now, to visit me.

A professor of English who was set to retire, a self-employed upscale furniture maker, the Doc, a couple of shop owners. I was meeting the townspeople. They all seemed to welcome me to their village. And they were filled with information about where to find the best food, clothes, people. I enjoyed the banter, the new faces, and watching them interact with each other. Many were opinionated about one another and the fires.

Grace had worked in several hotels at their front desks throughout her working years. She drove a Mercedes® like many people here I had noticed. I felt she was a widow. She brought the same man in once a week. He visited her from the south. They liked to sit at the bar, drink martinis on the rocks, and have fried oyster salads. Grace was very afraid that her sister's dress shop may be on the arsonist's list.

"It is amazing to me that no one has seen this person packing newspapers and gasoline. How can that be?" she protested. Henry stroked her shoulder.

Doc said, "Whoever it is, is a sly one, I'll give him that. I liked your article, girl," he complimented me. "It takes guts to waltz into town and taunt an unknown murderer. He may come after you!"

"I'm not hiding from a coward."

He laughed, but nodded in agreement. "You're tough, are you?"

"She's a mountain girl," Sharon from the trinket shop said, lifting her white wine to her lips. "Mountain girls know how to take care of themselves."

"That right?" Doc lifted his eyebrows.

I just laughed. I liked to listen and comment, learn, but not to reveal a lot about myself. Thankfully, in walked Erich.

Doc looked at me, then at Erich. "Wow. Haven't felt chemistry in a room like this in a hell of a long time. I prescribe a long walk on the beach!"

They all laughed at that. Luckily, I had to turn my back on them and make drinks for the service bar, and was able to compose myself. Erich waited. I could feel his eyes on me. "Hi, Doc. How's life with the sick people?" he asked.

"Still rolling in. I try to teach them to take care of themselves, but they seem to think that's my job," he laughed. Everyone snickered. "It's a living!"

"A great one, I'd say." Erich ordered a dark draft beer and a burger with onion rings.

"You want to go for that walk when you get out of here?" he offered when I laid his place-mat before him. I could see everyone at the bar perk their ears at that.

"Where's the beach?"

He ignored that. "We can take the Subaru® home first. Get Hank if you want."

"Sure. Sounds interesting." I tried to be cool while my knees shook, and I almost ran to the kitchen for no reason but to hide for a moment.

Knapps waved while docking the crab boat, as I left the restaurant with Erich. Knapps had said earlier that he wanted to see me. Show me some of his work. Talking with me had inspired him to do a bit more writing. Reading my paper seemed to really get him going. He must have decided it was important enough to interrupt whatever the P.I. was talking with me about. I could see that being a waterman was too tough. He hated the hours, the roughness of the men. It just wasn't his style, although being out on the water at dawn gave him a thrill every morning, the work itself was brutal. His Mom had told him for years that he must be who he is inside. That it is criminal to hide it away-God's gift to him should be shared with the world, cultivated. It seemed that he felt ready to plant the first seeds.

He tied the boat off and told Arnie he couldn't help any further that day. "Great," the crabber grumbled. "Ought a just work this boat myself. Dreamy-eyed kid."

"Sorry," Knapps smirked as he took off on a dead run to reach me. When he got close he slowed down to catch his breath so I wouldn't realize he was so anxious. He watched us as he approached.

"Pardon me, Cedar," he said from just behind us as Erich was opening my car door for me. I hadn't let on that I knew he was watching, approaching.

We both turned. "Knapps! Good to see you. Are you just getting off work?"

"Knapps? Wow. Remember me? You were just a kid last time I saw you at the family picnic," Erich gleamed.

"Hi, Erich."

"Geez. It's just like back home here. Everyone knows everyone and most are related," I noticed that they kind of looked alike.

"We are second cousins," Erich explained. "His Mom is my cousin."

"Figures!"

"Cedar, can I talk to you just a minute? I don't mean to interrupt, but…"

"Oh, sure," I said, curious now.

I took his arm and led him a few yards away so we could have a private conversation.   Erich sighed, "It was amazing how a lady could come to town and win everyone's hearts inside of a week," he said smiling.

Knapps rolled his eyes at him. "I wrote something I wanted you to read. That's if you have time. I know you are busy. I read your paper."

"I'm flattered, Knapps, and thrilled to know you are writing."

He blushed and handed me an envelope. "I'll talk to you later, okay?" he said, walking briskly away with his hands in his pockets, turning to wave to Erich before jogging off.

"What was that all about? The P.I. in me must know all things."

"Did you know your cousin is a writer?"

"I do remember his Mom mentioning something about that years ago. Is he any good at it?"

I shook the envelope at him," I'll know soon, but I have a feeling that he is. He just has never had the chance to let it shine."

"How do you know him so well already?"

"We met at the fire at Lumpy's my first night here. Morning actually. Hank ran over to him so I felt he can't be all bad. Next day he showed us around Tilghman. Met his Mom, too."

"Jesus, you waste no time."

"Life is short," I said getting into my car.

He held the door open just staring at me. I tried to act comfortable with myself. I was melting.

"OK. I'll race you to Railroad Avenue!" I yipped and tore

out of the gravel lot.

"You'll be meeting the town copper, then. It's 25 mph and they take it serious," he yelled.

"I'll chance it," I laughed out the window. But I was just kidding, and took time to check my mail on the way. No sense in letting him think he has become a priority.

Later, Iris just couldn't wait to tell me about this: Waiting next to his car, Erich adjusted his faded denim shirt, checked his rugged face in the side mirror. Big blue eyes stared at him. Straight white teeth gleamed. "I still got it," he mumbled, running thick fingers through wavy sandy hair.

"That right?" Iris laughed, knocking his knee out from under him from behind with her knee. He stumbled, humbled. They were both laughing, she holding two bags from the Village Shoppe.

"I'd offer to carry those for you, but my knee."

"Oh, I am quite capable," she smiled. " Iced tea on the porch?"

"Sounds good. Iris, how did you get to know Cedar?"

"Always the detective."

"Curious, she is quite a girl."

"I tend to agree. She is what you see."

" I believe that to be true. Was wondering if she has ever taken on any other arsonist/murders in print. I am worried."

"She had sent me a pile of her writings when we first started e mailing each other. She wanted to make sure I understood who she was. They are in the end table by the wicker sofa if you want to see them."

He was reading a copy of my paper from the summer of 2001. I had an editor's note that was telling the Ohiopyle State Park that in no way were their over-zealous rangers to over-step their bounds this year as they had the last. Innocent teenagers taken to the state police station in a sweep of the swimming hole, it seemed. They had physically shoved my niece into their car. I was working, and missed the commotion. Instead of questioning them there they took them to the state police barracks twenty miles away. In the "lowlands" it stated. I had put them all in their place at the time. With summer coming on again I was reminding them to steer clear of my family. The park had narrowly escaped a law suit by my cousin. They would not be excused a second time.

"Anything interesting in that rag?" I asked. He had been so engrossed that he hadn't heard me pull up. Hank was inside getting treats from Iris. Great watch dogs around here, I thought.

"Plenty."

I looked at him sitting there. Legs crossed. Eyeglasses propped halfway down his nose. He looked very intelligent, and irresistible. Almost. Hank and Ralph came running.

Hank pouncing for "Mom's" attention. "It's okay, Hanky. Mom wasn't gone all that long. I love my boy. You been sleeping the day away?"

Ralph nudged my leg with his huge head. Pawed me, knocking me into a chair, forcing me to pet him, too. "You're very popular," Erich grinned. "They didn't even bark when I pulled up and no one was here!"

"Their napping takes precedence to intruders," Iris said.

"Am I an intruder?"

"You know what I mean. You are definitely a welcome soul."

"We are going for a walk. Want to go with us?" Erich asked Iris.

"I think not. I have some paperwork to catch up on, but Ralph would love to join you if you don't mind."

"He can protect us from the criminal element of this burgh," Erich said, wincing, wishing he was kidding.

"Sucks, doesn't it? We never had a criminal element to consider before this. All these years of complacent relaxed life blown to hell by a firebug." Iris went into the kitchen, waved. "Have fun." She threw Ralph's leash to Erich. "I need to get to the library."

"I'll run upstairs and do a quick change if you don't mind," I said. "I'll be back in a jiff." Hank followed at my heels. I could feel eyes on me all the way up the stairs.

He went into the kitchen with Ralph already on the leash and pulling at him to go. I could barely hear them talking. "Did you read her papers?"

"Yes. She has guts, doesn't she?"

"I like that in a gal normally, but I don't have a handle on our culprit yet. Not sure they won't come after her for the article she wrote."

"She is a black belt in Tai Kwon Do. God help him."

"I'm ready to roll!" I yelled, running down the steps with Hank leaning against my legs.

"We better get going before he knocks you over," Erich laughed. "Why do they do that?"

CHAPTER 11

It's true that lots of people come here just for fun and that many move here. I'm sure the sheriff must have realized he could have a criminal in the midst who he spoke to everyday and not know it. Some minds were psychotic, great actors. But at least they could now watch for someone who rubs! Many came here to hide from one thing or another. The Eastern Shore was a great place for leaving the world behind. I know.

God, there were a hundred watermen who still chewed tobacco. Many rolled their cigarettes. Some of the retirement crowd, although upscale, were old fashioned, too. Then the younger ones loved to experiment with everything. Or it might just be a trick, or something that was there before the arsonist was. Who knew? The sheriff did not know. The press was killing him. The state boys wanted to take over. I felt that Erich was his only hope to keep peace and his badge. His deputies were coming up empty handed. They had been stopping people at both ends of town, and a couple of them had taken to riding bikes at all hours, looking, watching, trying to think like a psychopath.

And now Agnes was murdered. This was something that had to end and soon. Erich may come up with something more solid. It looked like his old friend did not trust his instincts as a lawman. He really had no instinct when it came to the criminal element. He just knew how to keep a village orderly. He was very good at that, and the residents trusted him to do it. Keep the noise down, the speeding to a minimum.

Rodney seemed to love his job as Postmaster. I watched him smile at every customer everyday I went in and now I knew who he was. He sold me a book of stamps. Let me put the papers in the lobby. He fixed his tie, grinned. Obviously feeling the women enjoyed seeing him each day-young and old alike. He always had a kind or funny word. And he looked good in the blue shirts they were required to wear. He must meet many travelers through his job, too. Everyone had to send and receive mail.

As I sat on the bench in front of the post office opening my mail he waved, throwing his right leg across a Honda® and revved her up. Just a few short blocks later he was chaining her to a pole at Poppi's. She was shiny, black, and his smile said he loved her. It looked easy to use, to putt around on. Scooters were popular now, too. You could buy them at the small mall in the middle of town, or even on the dock at the Crab House. They rented them, too. The older folks seemed to like those battery operated bikes. His had quite a bit more get-up & go. It was heavier, not that cheap plastic. And I noticed girls watching when they saw him (including myself). They wanted to ride it, no doubt, and he probably got a lot of dates because of it. I noticed him at Foxy's, the outside bar & restaurant below the Town Dock Restaurant, having fun with a few girls two nights ago.

I'd heard that the town wanted his home to tear down and rebuild a new police station. They had a brick building on Talbot Street, but wanted his property which is next to the library. They lived two blocks from Iris and I. I waved to him as I walked by with Hank most everyday.

Marci Lynn McGuinness

CHAPTER 12

Marley later told me about their escapades and it went like this. Iris and Marley sat in the captain seats in the back of the van while Dave drove. The back windows were tinted. They did not just stay in St. Michaels. They drove to Tilghman Island and back and Easton and back so that they would not be noticed so much. The girls watched diligently as Dave drove through back streets and alleys. What were they looking for? Anything unusual. They had different opinions on the type of person the arsonist/murderer was, but they agreed that he would not stop until he was forced to stop. Agnes loosing her life didn't scare him off. This puzzled Marley.

"Your average arsonist would lay back for a while if he killed someone, wouldn't he?" she wondered. "It's the fire that thrills them. Taking an innocent life is not a normal part of their game. This guy must have no conscience. None at all."

"He won't have a head when I get hold of his ass," Iris put in.

"We have to find him, look!" Dave pointed.

Two teens were walking through Freemont Street with a gas can. One was pushing a bicycle. "That's Chef's son and Roger Blaney's kid. They probably have to cut the grass today. They do a lot of that in this neighborhood for the older folks," Iris said.

"Watch them anyway. It could be anyone."

"I know, but in my mind it is not a young person. It is someone our age. Someone who is pissed at us all," Marley stated.

"That could be, but we'll park here a moment until they turn the bend." Dave headed into the back of the Acme behind the dumpster where they had a good view of the street that ran to the graveyard. The boys kept walking and talking, hats turned backward. When they turned up the back street, they all got out and walked nonchalantly their way, staying as far back as they could so they wouldn't be noticed. Many people walked in St. Michaels, but not back this street.

The boys stopped at an old worn garage, yellow paint peeling. Paul, the owner, came out and spoke to them. The three of them went over to an old BMW® and Paul opened the gas tank. One of the boys got in the car. The other poured the gas into the tank. "That's a relief," Iris sighed.

"Yeah, I don't want to have to rough up any kids.

even if they are firebugs," Marley said.

They walked back to the van and proceeded around the block only to see an old man behind the vacant building that once was a lady's clothing store. It was on the corner across from the Methodist Church. Jerry Hershey was remodeling the place, and paint cans and lumber sat inside. You could see through the front window. The man was on foot. They all knew who he was, had seen him around and spoke to him many times, but no one could think of his name. He stumbled and they slowed.

As he got himself righted, he looked the old building over, hands locked together behind his back like an inspector. His green work pants were a bit grimy. He stood that way for more than a minute before trying the door. "Hey," Jerry yelled from the upstairs apartment. Jerry waved him up, but the man shook his head in the negative. He waited for Jerry to come to him. They figured his knees were too bad to climb the steps. The men spoke for a moment and then entered the empty shop on the bottom floor.

"He's probably helping Jerry," Iris said.

"God, I thought we had our man there. I got the willies," Marley shook her head to try to get rid of the adrenaline that tried to surge through her at the thought of catching the arsonist.

"Let's get some grub, ladies, you game?" Dave asked.

"Starved and shook up. This P.I. stuff is not for the

light-hearted." Iris shivered.

"Erich doesn't know we are doing this, does he?" Marley looked at her friend.

"I sure didn't tell him." Iris assured her.

"He wouldn't like it. I can guarantee that," Dave said, "but we can't just sit around and wait for the town to burn to the ground."

I sat in the big wooden lounger with great fluffy cushions that were provided on the deck off of my bedroom suite. It felt good to put my feet up and wiggle my toes. I hadn't had time until now to read Knapp's work. It was a very busy Saturday night at the restaurant. My wrists hurt from opening dozens of wine bottles. My pocket was full of money, but I needed to unwind. The time had flown. The bar was full, but I had very little time to tend it as the waitresses and waiters kept me hopping, literally. I actually had to dart to and fro inside the small area that was my work space. There was no room for a manager to help me make drinks, so they rang up bar checks instead. People were in good moods for the most part, and it was all over by the time I even thought about the time. By 10:30 I was home petting Hank. This was late for Hank. At 9pm promptly every evening he curls up in a ball for a long night's sleep. Hank did not know about insomnia. A foreign idea. He sighed in my lap now. His "Mom" was home and everything was fine… except that I woke him. I read:

He was honest as they come on the outside, but I knew better. Since he came to town I always felt

*there was something wrong with the look in his
eyes. He smiled with effort, too. Like it hurt to
portray happiness when he was tortured inside.
People like that often fool the general public, but he
has never fooled me. He's nice enough to your face.
Polite. Always speaks, acknowledges you, but you
get the feeling his heart is not in his life here. That
he doesn't like anyone, really, just goes through the
motions for some unknown reason. To fool
everyone, I guess. To fit in when he knows he is a
bad seed. How does she not see it? I watch her
sometimes going to the bank, the post office, the
Acme. She looks like a happy fulfilled woman. She
looks him in the eyes everyday. Maybe she is so
happy with herself that she doesn't detect evil in
others even when it shares her bed.*

*I swear I saw him behind Lumpy's that morning.
The impression I got of a tall lean man was real,
but it was so dark. Am I sure? In my heart, yes. In
my mind, no. You can't just go around accusing
people on an impression, a feeling, a silhouette.
I struggle with this day and night. I watch him with
his wife around town. I must be wrong. Dead
wrong. I hope I am. I want to be.*

I folded the paper in my lap, wiping my brow. At
the top of the page he had called it "The beginning
of a story of fiction by Knapps Reckon."
"Fiction, my butt," I told Hank. "He knows
something. I knew it that morning, could feel it in
my bones."

I wrote a bit, then put the leash on Hank and went down the back steps. We ran the three blocks to Talbot Street where I could hear music from both bars. People stood outside smoking cigarettes. I hoped they could enjoy their evening without mishap. My mind reeled. Who did he see? He was reaching out to me, no doubt, but how did I get him to say the name when he wasn't sure? Was he sure?

Since she got that new cell phone he had no peace. She called to say she was almost home. Hell, she never went far, so why would he worry? She called to ask if Cole slaw was a better choice for dinner than salad. Thank God she could cook or he'd have to rethink their marriage. She was putting him into a tight corner. She didn't know it. Thought being in constant touch was intimate, loving. He was smothering as if he sat in a burning building and breathed the smoke into his lungs deeply. He read the paper, watched out the window. Cedar was coming by to pick up an ad later. She was a popular girl all of a sudden. He wondered why. And Erich McKnight was all but in love with her. Smitten, he would say, at the very least. A cold front moved in last night. He bundled up in his barn coat to take the morning stroll to Poppi's. He liked to talk with the guys at the counter, feel like he belonged. He never quite felt that way. Always lived within his mind. He chimed into conversations. Played the game. Was sure no one knew what went on in his mind. She didn't. She looked at the surface and liked what she saw. For an intelligent woman it amazed him that her intuition about him was so far off. Sure, he loved her as much as he could love a person. He wasn't romantic, but gave her attention, acted like he was listening, realized he needed her. He did know he needed her to look normal. If he was alone, a lonely man, he knew it would be more evident to people. The demon would rear its ugly head behind his eyes. Behind the forced facade he used when greeting people. He thanked God for his wife, and prayed he could keep her.

He pulled his hat down to ward off the powerful wind coming off of the water. Poppi's coffee kept lots of guys coming. Most wives thought they could make good coffee, but buying a popular brand was only the beginning. There was a technique to it, he was sure. Poppi's knew that technique. Everyone talked about it. And it brought them in droves. Anytime anyone asked where to have breakfast, to Poppi's they were steered.

He sat down next to the Chef from Town Dock. Even he liked their coffee. Of course, he did. He looked a bit worn. "Busy night?"

"You bet. Glad to have that new bartender, too. She kept things flowing."

"Looks pretty good back there, too, I'll bet," he smiled as if he cared.

Chef smiled and nodded. "It doesn't hurt, but she is fast, coordinated. Gets things done efficiently. The

wait staff loves her. That makes my life smooth."
"Smooth is good," he said putting both hands
around a large thick mug. He turned to the
newspaper. On page six a small column stated that
the investigation into the St. Michaels arsons and
murder continued. They did not mention leads.

I ran into Iris who relayed her visit to see her brother, to me. Erich sat at the kitchen table in his boxers, beer in hand. His mother was at her bridge game. He had some thinking to do. Coming back to the place you were raised is always an interesting thing. People are the same, basically. Some changes occur as far as real estate goes. People take on jobs and projects and marriages and have kids. But basically, the people are the same. St. Michaels and Tilghman have taken on a lot of strangers. It is this element that has both brought the old smelly oyster town into the real world with the well to do dumping their retirement money into the old houses and businesses, and bringing in an odd mix of personalities. It's not just the retired he was worried about. There were lots of people his age around who came from afar to play and hide on the Eastern Shore. That's how he felt about it. They couldn't be there to make their fortunes. There were really none to be made-unless you were in real estate. He laughed at that.

He lived in a Brownstone townhouse in Baltimore when he wasn't on his boat. Had bought up several of them around the downtown area. Hired a couple guys to fix them up. They did, and he leased them out to professional couples-childless. Some had small dogs, but his tenants were picked by the look in their eyes and their bank accounts. Being a Private Investigator was a good thing when it came to being a landlord. Not only could he check people out by the answers they gave him from his preliminary questions, they didn't even try to lie after they found out who he was. He had a reputation in Charm City. No one tried to cross Erich McKnight.

But on the Eastern Shore he was only read about. He had been a kid here. People didn't necessarily fear him. They respected him, wondered about him, felt him mysterious. He thought about how to flush out this culprit before any more damage was done. He hoped it was a stranger. Someone who had lived there long enough to be accepted as part of the town. Part of the woodwork. Someone no one feared. Someone no one noticed. That is the type who pulled this kind of crime. Someone screaming for attention. "Look at me. I can make you afraid. I can fool all of you. You are all dumber than me." He'd seen it a thousand times.

The last arsonist he busted was a woman. The police never looked at a woman for the crimes. Someone was burning churches. There was no rhyme nor reason to their pattern, and like this, someone finally got hurt. She had only struck at night. A lonely lady who had a crush on a Pastor who did not return her affections. She took it out on seven churches and one ill-fated homeless man who had been sleeping in a pew one unsuspecting night. He lost his life. She is in prison for thirty years now. Her drunken husband was shocked. He had ignored her for years. She wanted his attention, and that of the Pastor of the first church that burned. That is where Erich began his investigation. That is where he knew he would find the answers to that mystery. He finally sat next to her on the church steps of a small chapel in North Baltimore. She had been crying. It was so easy once he knew who she was. She just leaned into him, apologized for her crimes. He held her, sitting there for over an hour. When she was all cried out he took her hand and led her to his car. Bought her a hamburger at the drive through. She smiled. She was getting attention from a man. That's all she wanted.

Whose attention was this nut trying to get, he wondered? It was time to begin at the beginning. Iris. Her place was set on fire first, but put out. No damage done that couldn't be easily remedied. That was months before they finally burned her place down. Who wanted Iris's attention? A man? A lesbian? She didn't seem to know, had no other incidents besides the fires, wasn't seeing anyone.

Martha loved living in St. Michaels. She had felt at home almost immediately, and after several years, almost forgot about the stresses of city life that plagued most of her adulthood. Her husband, she

knew, missed the turmoil. His mind worked
differently than hers, but they had always loved
each other very much, and managed to be happy
together these fifty three years of married life.
Sometimes lately she felt him drifting away
mentally. Alzheimer's did not run in either of their
families, but she worried none-the-less. He was still
very healthy otherwise. A bit slower than before, of
course, but he did all his chores and was still the
gentleman she had met at the Library of Congress
where she worked all those years ago.

He had been a handsome young man, with dark hair
and probing eyes. She felt him watching her for
some time before she had the nerve to look his way.
But when she did look, her heart jumped. That was
it for her. She had never been on a real date before
and she was already twenty years old. Still lived
with her parents in Old Alexandria. She liked her
life, but knew that at that moment, things would
change for her. They smiled at each other. She
looked away. It was at least an hour later, or it felt
that long, when he came to her side and introduced
himself. He was a teacher just fresh out of college,
and looked so striking in his dark suit. She could
barely speak, so she tried a smile, blushed instead.
She was sweating from the emotions engulfing her.

"Might I inquire about your name?" he asked
politely.

"My friends call me Maggie, but I like Martha
better," she stuttered.

"I would like to be your friend, but I will call you

Martha," he had a slight smile. It changed his
solemn face. A face she liked instantly.

All she could do was smile back and offer her hand.
He brought it to his lips. Brushed it gently. She was
in love. They married four months later in a small
ceremony in her parents' gazebo. She was so
enthralled by his good looks, she felt she was living
in a dream. Some days, still, she could see her
young dashing fellow inside him. Some days she
missed him, watched as her husband dazed out the
window, unaware of her presence for hours. He was
still attentive, even at their age. She knew he
treasured her, and she, him, but things were
changing. He was not a very happy man anymore.
She had dreamed that St. Michaels would be good
for them both. Give them time to themselves-to
breathe, relax, just be. He was not good at just
being. He bored easily without a routine. Men were
like that without work to do.

He smiled across the table at her, "Penny for your
thoughts."

"I don't see any penny," she touched his wrinkled
hand.

"You were off somewhere."

"Just thinking about our lives together."

"Ah, the anniversary nears," he grinned. She always
relived their years when another one came to the
end, he knew.

"Really?" She got up from the table. Went around
and kissed his cheek. "I love you very much."

"You do, do you?"

They held hands. "Let's go for a walk," he offered. That they did. They discussed the town and the changes the fires were bringing. The fear and anticipation everyone felt was in the air. "Do you think we could spot the arsonist if we passed him?" she asked.

"I don't know that I ever met one, but how do you know it isn't a woman?" he asked.

" Ohh, really, do you think that is possible?"

"Anything is possible, my dear."

Marci Lynn McGuinness

CHAPTER 13

I was waiting for Knapps at dawn near the crabbing boat. He looked startled when he saw me. Happy, though. He seemed to feel a warm friendship toward me since I am a writer, too.

"Top o' the morning', Knapps," I waited for him to get to me. "I have a proposition."

"You're a morning person, aren't you?" he asked, rubbing the sleep from his eyes.

We both stood there thinking for a moment. I could see that Knapps was on pins and needles wondering what I was thinking about his story. He was shifting his weight from one foot, then the other. I was wondering who the hell he saw…or if it was fiction.

"You are quite the writer. Want a job?"

"Doing what?

"Helping me put together the newspaper. I'll need some competent talent, you know. I can do everything myself, I guess, but I would rather have the assistance of a good writer, someone who knows the area and people, someone who notices things." He turned red in the face. It was still dark out but I could see him blush under the street lamps. "Who did you see that morning?"

"I can't really say. I'm not so sure I was seeing what I think I was seeing. It could hurt good people if I was wrong…more if I am right."

"You have to say. This town is in major jeopardy."

"I know. I can't sleep thinking about it. I don't want to tell the cops yet. Can we look into it together to try to make sure somehow?

I looked at him. "Why don't you work with me, help sell ads, write some stories, help deliver the paper? Believe me, there will be plenty to do. I will keep what you know to myself until we are sure one way or another. Then we will have to tell Erich and the sheriff. If we are working together then people won't wonder so much about what we are up to if we do get to investigating a bit."

"You won't tell him before we agree what is real?"

"I promise we can tell him together when the time comes."

He held out his hand. We shook on it. "What do you want me to do first?"

"Go to work. Come see me after. I will be home after 2:30 today. Have to work at the restaurant. I'll pay you commission on your sales, and we'll come to terms later today about the other rates. You'll need to keep working on the water for a while until we get some money coming in to support this thing."

"That's great." He hugged me. "You are saving my life. I never thought I'd get to write for money. Everyone who has always thought I was just Knapps will know I can write. That is so cool."

"Your Mom will be happy, too. She has been wanting you to break out of your shell. I could tell."

"Yeah, she'll love it."

"We both will. Now spill."

He saw his boss approaching. "I'll have to tell you later, but not in Iris's house. Can we walk the dogs and talk?"

"That we can. Hank loves you."

He smiled and tipped his hat while he walked away, an obvious bounce in his step that I had not noticed before. No slumped shoulders this morning.

I watched as Gus pumped gas into the biggest yacht I'd ever seen. It was a beauty, like the lady who jumped off the bow and smiled his way. Dark wavy hair, early thirties, lean and tan. She must be the captain's daughter, I thought, until I saw the captain. He was older than Gus by a good ten years. Granddaughter, I hoped. A crew of four was working to get the boat ready to dock. It looked like they planned to stay a while. That was fine with me. The sight of that fine-lined yacht in the nearly deserted harbor was incredible, but it was pretty noisy on the dock with several work boats powering up. Then all was quiet as they motored away. Must happen every September. A three week slump before fall crowds converged, just like home. What a great time to visit here. It was warm, quiet, no traffic, no crowds in the stores or on the roads.

The lady thanked a crew member when he handed her a folded motor bike down the plank. She was on it and moving away, waving, before Gus had the tanks filled. Big tanks. I could see by the smile on his face that the lady and the sale made his day.

"I was hoping you'd stop by." he called to me as I approached. He had a good strong look in his eyes. Honest, smart, no-nonsense. "Girl, I'd sure try to marry you if I was a young buck."

The captain came on deck and allowed the crew to move the boat over next to the bulkhead. It must have been a hundred and twenty feet long. Gus had no slip to hold it. It was wide, too. I'd love to see the interior. Bigger than Gus' building, and much fancier.

"Good day, Captain," Gus said.

"That it is," the tall elderly man agreed looking at the horizon. "What a beauty." He sighed, "Did you see which way that gal went?"

Gus pointed toward town. "Looked to be in a hurry."

"Yeah, she's been anxious to look up an old friend. I hope she isn't making a big mistake," he mumbled, handing Gus his credit card.

"That's how we all learn," Gus mused.

"Some of us learn. Some repeat our mistakes."

"Must have been fun the first time." They looked at

each other. Two old men who knew a lot about life. I was sure of that. They both laughed for at least a minute. "Harold Gainer," the Captain said as he held out his hand. "And you might be?" he inquired as he offered me his hand.

"Cedar Jace," I grinned, noticing his handshake was still quite firm. A good sign, I knew. I liked the guy. Wondered how he made so much money. That yacht cost more than Gus' business would get even in this best of markets.

"She'll be back," Gus said.

"She always comes back. She's my grandniece, by the way. Raised her since she was five. Parents died in a diving accident. She's a good girl. Head strong, though."

Gus just nodded, head strong, he obviously understood. Harold walked toward his yacht, stretching slowly, looking around the harbor. He turned, "Where's the best place for breakfast? Nothing fancy."

"That would be Poppi's, a nice diner." Gus pointed toward the area where Poppi's was no doubt filling up with coffee junkies. Town Dock here is great, too, for lunch and dinner. Can't go wrong either way. Depends what you're looking for.

Harold nodded, walked toward the *Mermaid*. Disappeared inside. I hurried on my way waving to both of them.

Fire Chief Ramsey looked pretty bad these days, and obviously felt worse. They say that going to work had been what he always looked forward to every day. Marley said that he told his comrades repeatedly how Agnes made it a pleasure to get up in the morning. She loved him so much, and he loved her. They would wake smiling, holding each other, make love. As he showered and shaved she would make him coffee, poached eggs on whole grain toast, peel a grapefruit. She would either pack his lunch or he would come home and lunch would be ready - in the frig for him. Sometimes he ate out, but not much. It was always better if Agnes touched it. Always. She permeated the house. Her paintings hung on the walls. Her studio over the garage screamed with loneliness. She was an artist, did watercolors and sold them in the local stores. She illustrated children's books for local authors and publishers.

They had all been at the funeral, had sent flowers and cards, and came by their home periodically. She was evidently loved by many and had been a pleasure to work with, they told the widower. Agnes was a happy person-even growing up. She was born happy, always had her art. Who hated her enough to burn her up?

Iris said that when they were small children, Agnes would paint the skipjacks going out to dredge oysters in the morning. She sketched Randy's profile many times. The locals all knew she was irreplaceable and left a hole in his life he was sure would never be filled again. He looked desperate, ringing his hands, as I overheard his brother coaxing him.

"I just want to die."

"No way, brother of mine. Let's get out of here today, take the boat to Annapolis. I took the day off."

"For what?"

"A break. Let's go," Rodney said shoving him onto the sailboat.

They did go. I saw them taking off as I left the docks. Randy had not been back to work. He couldn't force himself. Took a leave of absence to try to make himself whole again-at least functional. Iris had mentioned that Rodney was worried about him. Was not sure he would not kill himself in a melancholy moment. They had a forty two foot wooden boat with a sleeper and a small galley and head. It had been built by their father. They had fished off of it a thousand times for fun. Their Mom used to pack picnic lunches and they all went out-the whole family. Agnes loved it and insisted on having a private wedding ceremony on the deck before their big reception. It had been lovely, and I'll bet the men had that day in their thoughts as they pulled out of St. Michaels harbor.

Rodney yelled at Gus who just came out of his shack. He pointed toward the way the girl went and Gus waved, nodded, pointed at the huge yacht at the bulkhead.

Later that day I saw that same girl walking toward the Acme behind Dave and a small hunch-backed old lady in front of me. I had known him such a short time, but his gait was evident even from two blocks away. It hadn't dawned on me that I was so hungry until now and I decided to go to the grocery store for some fruit and to check out the deli. I stepped onto the automatic door opener, a small basket on my arm. I started toward the huge Gala apples that seemed to be gleaming at me. Taking one in hand, I noticed from the corner of my eye that the stranger from the yacht appeared to be watching Dave as he and the older lady turned the corner of the far aisle.

My stomach flopped, sweat poured from my brow. What was going on? None of my business, really. He is a nice looking man. No reason she wouldn't look, right? But it was the way she looked at him that struck me. Gave me a chill, actually.

Maybe it is the refrigeration units making it chilly in here. I have a wild imagination. Danger around every corner and all that. Reading the signs above my head for the selections of foods in each aisle, I slowly proceeded toward the counter of the deli. I said, "Hello," to Dave and he introduced me to his mother-in-law. They were looking at paper towels. He held Bounty® out to her as she shook her head. He was a patient one, smiling.

The woman from the yacht was definitely looking at him fiercely now. Whew. Who knew what was what? I just moved here. Everyone's related. I knew how that was from home. Anyone could be up to anything.

Yes, I could see it. It excited me that there was so

much going on, plenty for both my newspaper and the mystery novel.

She looked at him as though she has thought about him for years They had unfinished business. I know people. You don't own a diner and write all these years and not learn people. A look in the eyes will tell you the story many times.

"May I have two pickled eggs and a half pint of Greek olives stuffed with blue cheese, please?" I asked the elderly lady over the deli counter, who smiled at me with an ornery grin on her face.

"You sure can, honey. You're Cedar, aren't you?"

"Yes," I smiled shaking the rubber-gloved hand reaching over the counter to mine.

"I'm Iris's Aunt Francis. She told me about you. Welcome to St. Michaels."

"Thanks. I am enjoying the Eastern Shore. It's been beautiful despite the fires."

Francis took a deep sigh and shook her head, going back to her work mumbling, "I don't know where it will stop. What is it they want?"

"Attention, that's for sure," I said taking the items and waving a good-bye.

He came up beside me without my realizing it.

"How are you two today?" Francis asked them as if she saw them most days at her job in St. Michael's Acme store.

Ruby's voice was shaky, but clear at the same time. "Pretty good today, Francis. How is that arthritis?"

"No complaints on a pretty day like this unless I have to wash pots!"

I couldn't believe what I was seeing, that girl seemed to just back around into the aisle just as Dave was about to turn and see her. She was not wanting him to see her watching him. Who is she to him? She scooted down the wine and beer aisle, as I turned to hear Dave order smoked turkey, Swiss cheese, and dill pickles. All of a sudden I saw him go pale and turn like he felt a ghost wisp over his shoulder—a double take. She went to the customer service checkout and bought cigarettes. There was no one in that line. Her hands were shaking, I noticed. She dropped the cash as she pulled a small wad of money from the front pocket of her cut off jean shorts.

"You okay?" the cashier asked.

"Low blood sugar," she whispered.

"You can sit across the street in the little park down there and catch your breath. You better eat something." She pointed to a few benches just two blocks down. Nodding, the girl escaped without being spotted. I checked out in the next station and saw her sitting on a bench, watching for them to come out, I thought. Weird. He helped the old lady into a green Ford Escort® station wagon and drove away, looking around the streets just before he got into the car himself. He felt that woman's presence, I knew.

CHAPTER 14

I stopped by to pick up Dave's ad as the sun rose because he said he was an early riser. Marley was in her country kitchen stretching like a cat, yawning out loud.

"Insomnia never plagued me like it does Dave. I sleep a full eight hours uninterrupted as if in a coma unless awoken by an outside force," she laughed, scratching her belly.

"I can attest to that," her husband agreed from the other room.

I could smell the strong brew from their automatic coffee maker. Simon wrapped his furry tail around her ankle, purred.

"What's up, Cedar?" Marley picked up the cat. Her question sounded mumbled as she talked with her face nestled into the thick coated charcoal colored feline. She held her up. "Wouldn't Hank like to tangle with you? Who would win that battle, I

wonder? Ah, not to worry. You shall never meet."
She slipped into her slippers and padded to the
living room with me in tow. "You have a visitor,
Hon. Seems our new resident publisher is an early
bird like you."

We found him on the couch with magazines and the
daily paper strewn about.

"Don't worry, I'll pick them up," he said realizing
his neat-nick wife would be appalled at the family
room's appearance.

Sitting next to him, she gave him a hug and looked
him in the eyes. You could see that she truly loved
him and liked living with him very much. That was
obvious. That first night she told me that she had
lived alone in a very nice apartment above an old
bank building on Talbot Street for over a decade
after high school. She had a hard time giving it up.
Everything was organized. The furniture was in
perfect condition. Book shelves lined the walls. She
had always been a bit of a loner, but he wooed her,
convinced her that two people who love each other
should spend their lives loving each other and
building a life together. A unit, he had told her was
better than being alone because being alone was
lonely. He insisted that he got lonely when she was
in the other room. Marley felt full of life with her
husband. She did miss the neatness of her former
household, but enjoyed loving her husband and
being a couple very much. It seemed to be a warm,
cozy, passionate relationship. They worked hard.
He went to car auctions twice a week. Sold good

cars at prices that both made him a nice profit and satisfied the needs of the locals. He also rented cars to sailors and the like. Vans, too. And he took her mother shopping once a week. A really nice guy. I handed Dave the ad I had whipped up. Seeing them together was interesting after watching that lady watch him yesterday. Wonder what was up?

"That looks great, Cedar. Let me sit down and give it a better look at my desk later today. When is the deadline?"

"You have a few days, but today works best!" We all laughed as I started out the door. "Are you two going to the town meeting this morning?"

"Oh, I forgot! Let me jump into my jeans and we'll be there in short order," Marley yelped.

Erich waited for me outside. When he took my hand, I closed my eyes for a split second. Heat rose through my body, my heart throbbed. I opened my eyes as he began walking at a fast pace, almost pulling me along. The dogs wanted to run-pulled us both.

"Looks like the meeting is already starting," he said as we approached. "How about we tie the pups out front for a bit and see what is going on," he said turning to face her.

He is so real, was all I could think. How could it be that I would move into this tiny village and in two weeks time, begin a newspaper, start a job, make wonderful friends, hire a writer, and meet a man who could make me dizzy just by being?

I just nodded and patted his chest. "I'm with you," was all I could say. He smiled at that, looking at me a moment. I knew he was reading into my words. We both felt the connection like electricity between us. Currents of lightening striking, is more like it. We then walked right into a heated discussion. Dan Crusar, the President of the town council, was telling the crowd of fifty or so that they had to organize to flush out the arsonist. When Erich held the door for me to enter in front of him, everyone looked our way. Marley and Dave were right behind us by then. Iris sat watching us stride across the floor to the seats behind her. Most everyone greeted us, except the President, who blushed. It seemed attention had been led away from his words. He had been a rival of Erich's as teens, I later found out. Always a bit nerdy, frail, laughed at. Now he was being upstaged by him again. I could hear Marley snicker as the President got red under his collar.

"If we could get back to the subject at hand," he said, calling the meeting back to order. "The arsonist/murderer could be in this room. We must face that fact."

"It could be you," Erich whispered a bit too loud-on purpose to get his goat. Again, Dan's blood boiled.

"I can assure you, it isn't me. Is there anything concrete you'd like to share with us Mr. P.I. or are you finished disrupting this meeting? Our town is under assault. It would help immensely if we took this seriously. A fire could spring up at any moment."

Marley stood. "He is right. Precautions must be taken and a plan carried out. A watch is organized somewhat, but must be twenty four hours a day seven days a week until this man, woman or child is put in jail."

"That is right," Iris agreed. "We are all afraid. They could start burning houses next. Who knows with a serial nut?"

"This town is made of wood. It is an arsonist's dream. We need to make it his nightmare," Dave said. "Let's get more organized so we can narrow down our focus. Does anyone have any evidence, suspicions that are almost solid?"

I thought about Knapps. I was sworn to secrecy and would keep my word, especially since I had yet to hear who he thought he saw. I felt Erich trying to read me. I refused to look at him. Turned so that my shoulder was toward his face. I faced Iris.

"A schedule of watchers for each section of town must be made."

"What if we schedule the arsonist?" Iris asked.

The sheriff walked in as she spoke. "Yes, what if you do and what are you doing?" Once again the crowd turned to the door. "A secret meeting? Am I an uninvited guest?"

"You're not the only one, my friend," Erich assured him.

"You people are scared, mean well, but need to leave this to the pros." the sheriff announced.

The crowd buzzed at that. "Nothing is being done!" Dave said. "I am not going to sit idle and wait until my wife has to put out a fire at my lot. It would be awful. All the fuel…and United Propane next door…" His words trailed as the group gasped out loud as if no one had thought of that.

Erich and the sheriff were going over a few background checks when I walked into the office. I listened. It seemed their suspicions were not pinned down to any one person, but they each had gut feelings about at least one person in town. They did not exactly agree or disagree…they were just trying to get to the bottom of things in a shaky situation. "Now we have these store owners all over town suspiciously staring at each other and everyone, day and night. It's insane." the sheriff continued.

"It might help stop the culprit for a while at least," Erich said, leaning against the window that allowed him to watch the main street, "but he may just get creative now. Pretty slick as it is, really. He has been at this for over four months."

"Don't remind me. Of course the first two fires were not considered serials. Iris's place seemed like a mishap. No damage the first time. Then the boutique didn't seem related. The kid had been doing some chores there, etc. It wasn't until the third fire that I realized we had a nut in our midst. You're the nut expert, my friend. How about you work your magic and get this town back to its normal harmony? We are not used to crime, as you know."

Erich continued to stare out the window. He

nodded, but was somewhere else. "Solving this crime, I hope," the sheriff nudged him in the shoulder.

"So many old people. God, I just feel they are so vulnerable on any given day. How must they feel now?"

The sheriff sighed, rolling his shoulders and neck. He was stiff and sore, had not slept for some time now. "What do you think of this one?" He handed Erich some papers with information on one of the people they were looking at for the arsons and murder. Erich read, keeping one eye on the street.

"Hmm. Anything is possible, but just because I don't like the look in someone's eyes doesn't make him guilty of all this."

"What does then? You have always worked that way-listening to your gut-putting lots of weight into the look in someone's eyes."

Erich stared at his friend now. He was home again and they expected him to save the town-be the hero. He wanted to wrap this thing up. Had things on his mind. Me. Baltimore. His aging mother. "It means a lot. You're right, but there has to be evidence to convict a person of this kind of thing. So far we are mighty short on evidence. Gas, charred newspapers. Even with DNA research today, fires are tough. Hair burns up. Plus, in shops, there are too many hairs and fingerprints to pinpoint one person to a crime like this. People go in and out all day long-even the back way. Delivery guys, relatives, dog walkers, plumbers. Hell, so many places have

construction and remodeling going on, it is
amazing."

"What do you think of that one, though. I never did
like him. Would love to get him out of this town. I
know he looks harmless. He's married to a
respected woman that everyone loves. He has never
done anything wrong. Doesn't even drive over the
speed limit, doesn't drink outside his home that I
know of. He just seems secretive to me."

"People are entitled to their secrets."

"Depends what they are, Erich."

I cleared my throat and the men finally realized they
had company. "Sorry, you were engrossed there."
He knew that was very true. Wondered what secret
this one held that the sheriff feared. Didn't see him
as an arsonist, but in a tiny town where most
everyone was of one class, wore the same chinos
and navy sweaters, it was damn hard to pick one nut
from another. Who would move to a clickish place
like St. Michaels only to slowly burn it to the
ground? What is the purpose? Who are they so
angry with? Could it be Iris they want to hurt?
Could they be trying to cover for an ultimate
insurance payment on their own property?
Something just didn't add up. By now someone had
to have seen something. Why is no one coming
forward?

He came out of his stooper and looked at me.

"I have a lunch date with Cedar."

" A date. Is that what we're doing?" I looked him
over.

I seemed to make him babble like a teenage boy. I
liked that very much. I smiled at him like the cat
who ate the canary. But did he have time for love?
Was he interested in love? We knew the chemistry
was so very real, but what next? We weren't kids.
Had lives and goals of our own. And I was stirring
things up with my paper. I was working on
something right then that I wasn't telling him about.
God, did I know something that could be of help
here? No, not yet, that is for sure. I wouldn't allow
people to be hurt.

"I better keep an eye on you two," the sheriff
claimed. "It's hot enough in here to start a fire."

"We heard," Erich told him and turned to me. "How
about a bite to eat? We could use a good look-see at
Poppi's. Listen to the people. See what is up. I
really feel that something is brewing here that we
are not aware of. Who do you think is pissed
enough to pull this off?" he asked the sheriff.

"Hell, what is there to be pissed at? I picked up that
Marks boy for going through people's trash.
Stealing people's identities is what he was trying to
do, but he didn't have the smarts to go through with
it all. He was gathering up some info, though. Sure,
he'd be mad, but not capable of this. He would have
been caught the first time out. Then there are the
druggies. We pick them up on occasion, but they
are small time, too, and not violent like this. I feel
like it is someone who is not content more than
angry. Someone who isn't getting what they need
here. ..or hates the small business owners. It seems

thought out. This person is wise."

"Who has the association ticked off lately?"

"I've thought about that, but it is also small stuff. Fights about when to have garbage picked up. Bed and breakfast ordinance arguments. Stuff like that. Sometimes they argue about what is allowed in the visitor's center hut. Who would go through all this over those issues?"

Erich opened the front door. We walked out into the bright sunlight. As he took my hand I saw that Knapps was walking down the street a block away. He called for me to join him. I wanted to see what he wanted. He still needed to tell me what he thought. "I'll just be a minute," I told Erich. I need to speak with him."

"What is up with you two?" Erich asked.

"Writers," was my only answer. The sheriff raised his eyebrows as he stepped through the door. He's known Knapps since the day he was born. Bet he never knew he was the brainy type.

I laughed out loud, spit a bit, too. He was not only brainy, he was entertaining. Suddenly I whipped around-had felt eyes upon me even though I had been very much into our conversation. Those vibes coming toward me were strong. He had held my hand. Intimate was the only word I thought of when he did that. I felt his heat through that small but possessive gesture. People who love each other hold hands, I knew. Liked my new life here very much. Wanted time to be myself, on my own. I had been raising Willie for fifteen years. Ran the business night and day. Found his killer and dealt with him. Grieved for years. I had dreamed of living on my own. Being Cedar. Writing, finding my way as Cedar, not someone's mom or someone's wife. Love should not be all-consuming. But my experiences with it drove me to yearn for freedom. I needed to be admired by men, but to have my own life. I felt I was building a good life here already. Making friends, working on my novel, developing a newspaper. So much to do. Why was he so damn handsome? Why did his dark eyes make me jump into the air with glee? Why did I feel it so strongly when he was within a mile of me?

"Him again!" Knapps shook his head. "He has it bad for you, Cedar."

"You think?"

"You know it, too," he pulled my arm around the corner and we walked into Flamingo Flats. Pretended to be looking at the books on the racks, the spices. "What if I told you I don't like him very much?" he asked.

"Is that true?"

"No, he's okay."

"You sure? Do you know something I should know?"

"Only that he is intense."

"Like you, you mean? You need to tell me what you saw."

"It looked like Dave. The walk, the clothes, but he wore a hood and it was dark."

I stared. "Marley's Dave?"

He just shook his head slightly in the affirmative as if he could hardly stand the thought himself.

We exited the shop just as the sheriff and Erich walked over. We fell in behind the men. Quietly. No one said a word. The four of us just walked along. Crossed the road to Poppi's, took a table together. Looked each other over.

"Knapps," the sheriff nodded finally. "How is your mother?"

"Good, I guess, Sheriff." Knapps smiled. Everyone smiled now. "Any luck on the fires, yet? She's real worried. Misses Agnes bad. It's hard to see her so sad. I miss her, too."

"I hear you're a bit of a writer, Knapps. How did I miss that all these years?"

Knapps shrugged his bony shoulders. The waitress saved him from answering, and we all ordered our lunches.

"Okay," Erich said. "What are you two up to? Seems you have had your heads together about something."

I looked at him. Was thrilled to be across the table from him, but also happy he was not next to me. "Business."

Erich nodded. "Any chance I can get an ad in your paper?"

"Sure there is. What are you advertising? 'I spy. Don't lie'? That will get them calling!" I was almost dizzy with adrenalin…or silliness. I wasn't sure which. The information Knapps dumped on me

had put me into some kind of shock. When Erich was near I had a hard time being myself. I averted my eyes, but had to look at him when he said, "Something like that. What will that cost me?"
I handed him a folded sheet of paper that had been in my back pocket. It was my advertising rate sheet. "Knapps, you going to work for Cedar?" he inquired.
"That I am, Erich. That I am." Knapps looked like he wasn't sure what was happening to him. He seemed older. Was not so intimidated by Erich like he had been as a kid. Leary, maybe.
I could see that Knapps felt Erich could see through him and didn't want him to read his mind right then. He and Cedar had things to figure out. When their specials came he woofed his down in record time.
"We better get going, Cedar." he said pulling my elbow. "An appointment," he nodded at the men and then the waitress so she would get their check. I went along, interested to see what would happen next. Men were very interesting if nothing else.
I excused myself and told Erich I'd meet him at the saloon for happy hour if he would like to have a real date without these intrusions.

At home, Iris was walking the floor talking on the phone to the insurance company. She barely acknowledged Knapps and I when we entered the front door. Knapps stepped back onto the porch, signaling that he would wait for me there.
I went to get the printout of a mock paper for the

next edition. We were wanting to get one out by the
first of the week. My own phone upstairs was filled
with messages from business owners who wanted to
advertise. I would return their messages, train
Knapps on what to do to collect their information
and checks, and get this thing on the stands before
another fire hit. I decided to run the first chapter of
my novel as a serial. Then as I got it completed I
could either sell it to a bigger publisher or self
publish it. Maybe sell movie rights. I was getting
ahead of myself in my mind. Had messages from
both my sisters who I would touch base with later
that evening.

Both dogs had Knapps cornered when I got back to
the porch, forcing him to pet them. "You seemed a
bit nervous at lunch," I said.

"You, too," he laughed. "He gets to both of us, I
think. What is it about him?"

"Intensity!" I steered his attention to work by
handing him the papers so he could see the layout.
The headline was about "Fall into St. Michaels."
This was a promotion the business association ran
each year to get people to the little town to enjoy
the season and spend their money. I wanted them on
my side. It meant everything for the success of the
paper. I handed him a digital camera. "Do you
know anything about photography?"

"I took a class in school. Liked it, too. I think I can
take some good shots. Never used one of these,
though. I have looked at them. They seem pretty
easy to use."

"Is your computer pretty up-to-date? I forgot to ask."

"It's not fancy, but pretty new. I got it on a clearance sale. Saved up. Have to have the internet, you know. And I like to play some games, too, so it has plenty of power."

"Well, good. You can to add this ACT program to your system. It will make our work much easier if we are using the same program. It is the database you will use to list your customers information and notes about your conversations. Great tool. You have Microsoft Word, right?"

"Yep?"

"You'll need that. What about your internet program? Send me your e mail and contact information and I'll get you some cards made."

"Cool. The paper is going to be cool, too, Cedar. I can hardly believe I got this lucky. To meet you and everything, I mean."

"Who's getting lucky?" Marley asked stepping up onto the porch.

"Jesus, you scared me!" I jumped.

"Walk like an Indian, and the dogs don't bark at me."

Knapps just looked at her. He had confided to me that he was never sure if he liked her. She seemed kind of masculine in his eyes, but he knew she was married. Wondered why any woman would want to fight fires. Hell, if he was a woman, he would have a clean job, he said. Something interesting…like writing. I reminded him he did and he was a guy.

"What are you two up to here?" Marley asked
looking over Knapp's shoulder to see the papers he
was holding there. "Everyone is all a-buzz about
you, Cedar. They have needed a place to advertise
and say their piece for a long time."

"I am going to let them do just that in this issue. I'll
have quotes about the fires. How people feel. Any
suggestions on that note?"

Iris joined us with a tray of iced teas. "This the
strongest you got for Lois Lane and Clark Kent
here? They may need some real reinforcements
tackling this topic," Marley egged her.

"Any news?" Iris looked at her friend, concerned,
tired.

"No news, just thoughts. Everyone seems guilty to
me lately. It could be almost anyone, and no one,
you know?"

Emails kept me busy early evening. My sister's kids
were loving school, but kids always have dramas to
solve, and their Moms were the kind of mothers
who were always there to help solve their problems.
I helped, mostly by listening and asking questions.
They often came to conclusions just by being led to
them. They always told me how much they loved
and missed me. Missed me being there in the diner.
Said the new owners took crap from people. I had
our mother's way of putting people off with a few
choice words in the right killer tone of voice. I
smiled to myself, thinking of how the locals must be
treating the poor newcomers.

I needed a break, so Hank came along for a walk. I
had not been paying attention as we walked down
the quiet dead end street that led to the river.

A man stepped from behind a brown rental house,
which was empty if the "For Rent" sign was any
indication. There was still a little light, but the street
lamps did not shine in this area. He looked at me
intently. I recognized him immediately even in the
dimness.

"I didn't mean to scare you," he said in a low voice
as he came up beside me. Hank growled and
snapped at him. He kicked at the dog and teetered.
Grabbed my elbow so he didn't fall. He seemed to
have something to say and I did not want to ruin the
chance. I felt he had no weapon and knew I could
hurt him easily if need be. I wanted information. "I
know you are writing another paper. I want you to
say you interviewed someone who says he saw all
those fires."

"Did you?"

His eyes seeped. They were red with age, worry. I
was sure he was a bit mad. It showed in his
unkempt clothes. Hank had him on point, a low
warning coming from his throat.

"Are you saying you started all the fires here, killed
Agnes?"

"I am tired. All I want is a voice. I promise you."

"I'll need my tape recorder."

"No, no tape. Just ask me a few questions here. If
you're good at what you do, you'll remember
exactly what was said."

We faced each other now, standing only a few inches from each other's faces

"Did you set all the fires in St. Michaels?"

"No, and I didn't kill anyone."

"What is your point then?"

"Generations ago my family owned a few front street buildings. My brother let them go to auction because he wouldn't pay taxes. Stubborn as Dad. So I am enjoying this a bit. Sue me. I am bored, frankly. Maybe the first one was really an accident, then they couldn't help it. No one was getting hurt. People got their insurance money."

"Did you see someone set all the fires?

"I will not admit to that to anyone."

"I am a writer. You need to speak with the sheriff. Did you know Iris's father?"

"Of course." He let go of my arm. I knew now that he held on to me that whole time to keep himself from falling.

"I can't print this. What would I say?"

"Murder in St. Michaels," he sneered while walking into the darkness around the corner.

I watched him go, then turned and ran to Main Street. Erich was just pulling into a parking place to go to the saloon. He stopped. I got in. "Hi, beautiful What's up? You look like you've seen a ghost."

I shook my head. We went into Carpenter Street Saloon and he bought me a Guinness® beer. At the corner booth upstairs where the karaoke was just beginning, I relayed the encounter around the corner. He said he would find and interview the man first thing in the morning. "Maybe he does know, but why not go to the sheriff?"

"He said he was enjoying the show, but Agnes, I think, stopped it from being fun."

"Let's dance," he said taking me by the hand and pulling me close. Our bodies fit so well together. He looked down into my eyes, kissed my lips softly. He held me so close. Watched my eyes for any hint of hiding things from him.

"I've seen him before. You know I don't know everyone like you do. He didn't give me his card, but I know you know him. I'll point him out tomorrow."

He stepped back, twirled me to Dave Mathew's "Crash into me." We danced through three songs before returning to our booth. The crowd grew thicker. Groups of friends grabbed tables and sang together, laughing. It reminded me of my home, my friends. I had sung karaoke many times-not well, but happily. Now we looked at each other. I had wondered when he would REALLY kiss me. I liked it, but was so wound up from the confrontation in the alley. Not too much too soon. Soft lips. I was smiling at him, didn't want to talk about the fires.

"I feel like you and Knapps both know something about these fires that you are keeping from me."

"Let's please just enjoy the music. You just kissed me."

He finally smiled at me. Dark eyes boring into mine. "I wanted to do that the first time I saw you at Poppi's."

"Is that right?

"You are avoiding my question, I believe."

Someone belted out "Mustang Sally" and I was on my feet. Dancing felt good. It had been too long. He joined me. The place was old and small, but people filled the entire building enjoying their beer and each other's company. This was one of a few taverns in the tiny burgh. He grinned as I moved around the dance floor. He was obviously enjoying the sight of my snug capris on my firm behind. I felt good cutting loose. That old man did scare me at least a little bit although I showed no outward signs of the wobbly knees now.

Erich admired me, I could tell, but feared I may be reeling in the bad guy right under his nose. I thought that he felt he was slipping. Was not being of much help in this case. What was it he should be doing? He wrapped a strong arm around my waist and pulled me into him.

"Tell me now or I am leaving."

We stared at each other a moment. "An ultimatum. Wow! We're not even married. I don't adhere to threats. Have a great evening." I stepped out of his grip, picked up my beer from the table, took a long swig, and placed the empty on the bar on my way out the door. Hank was waiting patiently by the stoop. We ran all the way home. Iris was sitting by the pool in the moonlight.

"Have a swim," she yelled as I ran up the back stairs. I waved and went in to change into my suit. I told Iris about the man and about Erich. Hank peed in the neighbor's yard, then jumped into the warm water and swam with me. Ralph barked at him. Wanted to save him. Iris made him stay. "He will drown you both if he gets in. He thinks you are going to drown and he tries to save everyone, but ultimately hurts them every time. He is far stronger than he knows. Enjoy your swim. Ralph, be a good boy and stay." He groaned, lay there watching them play.

"You have to describe this man to a tee for me. I am sure I know him."

"He looks so much like so many other older men around here it is remarkable.

"Yes, and it looks like Erich has it bad for you."

"He sure has some soft lips…and I am sure he was pretty surprised when I left him in the bar. Why do men feel they always have the right to rule us? Amazing to me that a man I barely know gives me ultimatums. That's crap."

"He is afraid for you, you know. This person or these people are not to be toyed with. He thinks, knows you are in danger."

"From him, I'd say."

Iris laughed and rolled her eyes. "Knapps dropped off an envelope for you. He looks like a whole new kid. It is amazing. Said he sold quite a few ads today."

"God bless him," I said pulling myself up out of the pool and grabbing Hank's collar to quicken him up the steps to the deck. "That felt so good. I am so happy to be here with you, Iris. I can't tell you how at home I feel. I don't want to put myself or anyone in danger at all. I am only a writer. He came to me. He was afraid, more than anything, I think."

"Did you believe him…that he saw the arsonist?"

"That's not exactly what he said. He only hinted and left me wondering."

"That's too much. Who could it be and why?"

"That is the question," Erich approached quietly from the side street. "Nice guard dogs you have there."

CHAPTER 15

I tossed and turned all night. So much had happened
lately. I thought that leaving my home, family, and
friends for a new area would be a long tough
adventure. A long road to hoe. Even my wild
imagination had not shown me the reality I was
living today. Who could really be burning all those
quaint shops? And why? What a touristy town for
this to happen to. I had been looking at their web
site and hearing stories about the place for years.
Dreamed of a peaceful life among peaceful people.
What a dream! Fires, a murder, Erich, Knapps, a
new job, a new newspaper, an old man sneaking up
on me in the dark side street, an ultimatum from a
man already, whew! It was a bit much for only two
weeks. So much had not happened to me in such a
short time since they found Willie. Hank was curled
up in a tight ball at my feet. This hound dog was the
one sane thing in my life.
I had been dreaming all night. This one was the

worst. Iris and I wore tool belts and boots, cut off jeans and tank tops. We were working to rebuild Lumpy's on our own. Iris no longer trusted anyone. The building was block. There would be no wood. "Just try to burn this baby," she said leaning against her truck. I laughed, lit a cigarette (I have never smoked before in my life). Men rode by all day whistling at us, stopping and offering their assistance in many ways. We shooed them away. Marley pitched in on her lunch hour, but we shooed her husband away, too. Iris was rude to him. He seemed to annoy her. She had confided this to me in the dream, but not in real life. Hank jumped out of bed barking and I woke in a shot.

"What is it, boy?"

He was at the sliding glass door. I stumbled to it and let him out on the deck. Iris was skimming the pool while Ralph swam. How could she get all that dog hair out of it? We ladies waved at each other. I sat back down on my bed. Laid back and closed my eyes trying to force the dream back into my head. I could see us at Lumpy's, but there was something I knew I just had to remember that wouldn't come forward. Hank was on the bed then, licking my face rapidly.

"Okay, okay, I'm getting up. I'm peeing before you, though." I rubbed his head. He jumped to the floor and ran in circles after his tail. I had rescued him from a family who tied him to tree as a pup and never fed him or gave him water. There were four kids and two parents and they all ignored this neat little pup. A neighbor took the dog from them and talked me into taking him when she figured I needed a buddy. I loved him deeply.

"Let's go," I laughed as he pulled on my shorts and t shirt. "Who wants to run?"

Hank was so excited. We ran down the road waving at Iris. Hank watered many shrubs and did his business in a patch of woods. Then we ran non-stop for a mile until we came to the water at the end of Railroad Avenue. Running made Hank so happy and helped to clear my foggy mind, but he had to stay on the leash. He loved to hunt and could run for hours after a scent. I learned to keep him attached to me for the most part. We walked back giving me time to think about my day. Erich would have to be dealt with but in the meantime I had a paper to write and layout and a job to get to. I really loved the evening shift, 4-9. I usually came home with a nice wad of cash in my pocket. All was right with the world…or was it? Erich pulled up alongside us.

"Stalking me? I believe that is illegal, Columbo."

"So is withholding information on a felony. The sheriff wants to see you, beautiful."

I glared at him. "You really know how to wow the ladies," I said sarcastically and took off running. He was there waiting for us when we returned home.

"Tell the sheriff I'll answer any questions he may have as soon as I get some things done around here. How's noon for him do you think?"

"The sooner the better," Erich said and pulled out of the driveway.

Iris watched the exchange. I'm sure we were a curiosity to watch. Broke the boredom of her own non-existent love life at the moment. "Coffee?" she asked, handing me a mug when I came in covered in sweat. We just looked at each other and laughed.

"Tell them what you know even if you aren't sure you know it, Cedar. It might help."

"What is it they think I know, I wonder?"

"They are having a difficult time with this. Grasping at straws. You might have instincts that would nudge them in the right direction of the investigation."

"Anything to help stop this insanity and get to the peaceful life I came here for," I said going up the stairs to my computer.

"Maybe we can take a walk later," Iris called after me.

Knapps needed some wheels. He said that he was so very tired of hitchhiking and feeling like a child, bumming rides. He had saved his money, but wasn't ready to take on the expense of car insurance and maintenance. Just past the draw bridge his cousin sold boats, bikes, and whatever he could fix up for a profit. There that morning sat a Moped®. On the island the old men rode these every day. They went fast enough and you needed no insurance to get one on the road. He had been saving up for a couple years, but still didn't want to spend all his money. Knapps was a frugal kind of guy. I had heard some say that this is why he didn't have a girlfriend. He threw his right leg over the seat and pulled the handlebars up. It felt right. And he liked the bright yellow color.

"Well now, Knapps, you ready to get yourself some transportation are ya?" Russell Martin said as he moseyed out of the garage. He had a toothpick in the corner of his mouth which he rolled around, as usual. Knapps thought he had never seen him without one and wondered if he slept like that. Expected he would die from splinters in the throat making him bleed to death or choking in the night. He wondered if he took it out to brush his teeth or kiss his wife. Judy came out on the porch. She was really pretty. Knapps never understood why she stayed with his grumpy sloth of a cousin. Couples confused him.

"You give him a good deal on that bike now, Russ," she yelled.

Russ mumbled and waved her away.

Knapps smiled at that because Russ had a reputation as a tightwad...much like himself. Judy had a good job with the tourist bureau. She wasn't home much. That may have helped save their marriage. He smiled. "How good is the motor, cuz?"

"It was never ridden much. Like new. I didn't have to do anything to it but clean it up a bit. How about $1200.?"

"That's probably not the deal Judy was talking about," Knapps prodded.

"Damn woman ought a stay out of my business."

"I can give you $500."

"What the hell you trying to do to me, boy? You a thief now?"

"I bet you paid less than that for it. I know you, remember."

That brought a smile to his face. He had taken Knapps with him to a couple auctions as a boy. Big mistake, he probably thought now, but had to be tickled the boy got something out of the experience. "How about $850, then?"

Knapps smiled and haggled a bit more. It was fun making the deal. He knew he would spend only what he wanted to that day. After handing Russ $600, he rode off on his new motor bike. He called her Sunshine. The ride to St. Michaels took about twenty five minutes going full tilt. He enjoyed it immensely. People waved and honked their horns at him. It was his day off from the boat, but he was going to town to let me know that he sold a couple ads on the island…and to show off his new bike. As he passed the lot where Lumpy's used to be, he slowed and remembered that morning. It was so dark then, and he only saw them out of the corner of his eye. He was sure he should tell the sheriff, but definitely didn't want anyone to know he did, especially if he was wrong about what he thought he saw. As he proceeded up Talbot Street he saw me walk into the sheriff's office. His heart jumped into his throat. He broke out into a sweat, worried that I would reveal his secret.

He rode by as slowly as he could, parked next to the building and sat on the bench, thinking. Should he

go in? Should he wait for me there? Should he go
see what is going on? He took several deep breaths
and walked back the side street to think a bit more.
All of a sudden he hit the ground hard landing on
his face. He was unable to catch himself, he had
been in such a state. A foot had tripped him. As he
took in the sight, he realized a dead man had tripped
him. An old man. He ran to the sheriff's office.

"Knapps?" I said just staring at him as he burst
through the glass door.

"Can I help you, boy?" the sheriff inquired.

"I think you better come out here. There is a dead
man in the alley," he sputtered, falling into the seat
beside me.

Knapps blurted, "I also might have seen the arsonist
that burnt down Lumpy's."

Erich looked at me, then Knapps.

"Take a minute and tell us what you know. It could
really help break this case and save this town, you
know?"

"There's a body that knocked me over!" He
screamed at the P.I. as the sheriff flew out the door.

Marci Lynn McGuinness

CHAPTER 16

The headline and leading story of my newspaper read:

"*Who and Why? Residents Cry!* Local law enforcement officials fight to find their arsonist/double murderer (or are there two murderres?), after discovering the body of St. Michaels resident, George Faith, lying face down on Carpenter Street with a large bump on the back of his head. The official cause of death is heart failure, but the man's condition shows that he was attacked.

'Fall into St. Michaels' sees business booming compared to last year's sales. Shop owners, restaurants, and charters report all time highs in their cash registers and are excited, but still fear that fire or fatality could strike at any moment. Who could be causing this phenomenon? Why would they do it? St. Michaels is well known for having a very low crime rate. Now, the fires and murders have caused the curious to visit in droves, spending money in stores they fear may literally disappear before the Christmas season. The spring was an exceptionally rainy one. Summer had been slow with extremely high temperatures and thick humidity. The loses local businesses incurred during their normally high season are being made up and then some, they say."

We were sitting at the bar in the Town Dock and everyone was all abuzz about the article and firing questions at me, commenting, talking over each other. I was forced to pour a dark draft just to take it all in.

"The business association dumps all their advertising dollars into 'Christmas in St. Michaels' that no one came this summer. The weather was so hot and humid, people couldn't walk the streets and shop anyway. So they had forgotten about us. No ads anywhere. People have short memories. Do you think the store owners are starting the fires themselves? Oh, my God!" Stephanie blurted.

"Hey, you are taking this thing way out of context and jumping to dangerous conclusions," I had to interject. "This is getting out of hand. No one in authority thinks that, I am sure."

I was happy with the story. It went on to say that at least two people have come forward anonymously with information. It reported that the Sheriff's Office was looking into evidence to see where the facts lie. I promised to keep everyone apprised. In a separate editor's note I thanked everyone for their support in getting the newspaper off to a strong but scary start.

"And look at this story written by Knapps Reckon. Doesn't he work with one of the crabbers? I see him hitching rides to Tilghman a lot," Kevin declared. "He found the body and was wanted for questioning before that, I heard."

"Okay, that's enough," I said. "I'm beat. Stayed up all night writing and printing that thing. I'm going home."

Smoke rose from the marina the next morning as Knapps parked his Moped. He had stayed at his cousin's the night before so he didn't have to ride so far in the middle of the night to get to the boat on time. He was being more careful now that he found George. He wasn't sure he was out of danger himself.

Many of the men cooked aboard, had smokey diesels. He rubbed his swollen eyes trying to wake up for a long days work when he realized there were flames coming from the *Gladys*. It was his turn to get things going this morning. No one was aboard as far as he knew. He ran, tried to get the hatch open. It was hot as hell. He threw the boards aside in a fit of temper and flames shot out at him. He grabbed the fire extinguisher that was stashed in the locker on deck. He knew in his heart this was no accident. That the arsonist didn't like his involvement. Small towns. Nothing got by anyone, except this bastard. As I came around the corner with Hank, Gus jumped aboard with his own extinguisher. He had seen the flames from the window of his apartment above the boat shop.

A fire whistle blew, but it was all over by the time the trucks arrived. Marley stood with her hands on her hips; spit on the ground. "Now this has got to stop!" she practically screamed it. Randy shook his head. He smelled the gas, the newspaper before he even stepped on deck. Arnie showed up just then. Took off his hat, rubbed his head.

"How bad is it?" the waterman asked the fire chief.

"Looks like it was set as a warning. Everyone knows when you guys get to the boats in the morning. If they wanted to destroy her completely, they would have set it an hour ago," Randy said.

Knapps kicked the ground. He was next to Marley now. "This is too scary for me," he mumbled.

They walked away from the crowd. "Oh shit," she said. "What did you tell the sheriff?"

"I am not allowed to say. The sheriff and Erich are investigating."

Just then the sheriff arrived. He took Knapps aside for questioning. Gus followed. "Sheriff, I saw someone over here earlier. Couldn't sleep. Didn't pay attention. It's not unusual for men to be here in the middle of the night."

"Think hard, Gus. That could be our man."

Iris showed up in her hot pink satin pajamas, red hair flowing. Hank followed Knapps who bent down so his friend could lick his face. We ladies waited until the sheriff let Knapps go. I threw my arm around his shoulder and walked him away.

"You okay?"

"I'm pissed now. Can we put out a special paper? I want to lore this bastard into a trap. I've been thinking."

Erich arrived and ran to them in his jeans and golf shirt. God, he was handsome, was all I could think when I looked up seeing his mussed hair. Just fell out of bed on Tilghman Island, I knew. That's why he was ten minutes behind everyone. The sheriff came over and asked Knapps to get into the ambulance. He refused. Said he was not burnt bad enough. We girls took him straight to the house and rinsed his arms in cold water, had him put his face in a sink full of it, too. Then we applied Aloe Vera gel.

"That feels cool," he smiled.

Iris handed him a cup of coffee. The sun was rising as Erich put his strong hand on the boy's shoulder.

"I called your Mom. She is on her way. I think your information was closer to right than you figured. You two need to lay low while I head things off. No matter what you see or hear me do, please do not question me and keep your mouths shut. You can report on the facts. That's all. I am going after this fucker."

He got up abruptly, kissed me on the mouth and walked out the door. We all heard him sigh deeply when he stepped out onto the porch before getting into his car and driving back to the marina. Television vans and reporters crowded the streets. It was rumored that the governor was coming in for a conference. I sent Knapps off with his mother who promised to take him across the Bay. I ran through the side streets to join Gus and his pals on the bench. He had made a vat of coffee and passed it out to anyone who approached them, which was plenty. Photographers took live shots. So did I. Cameramen and women filmed the old timers. "In all the years you have been meeting here each morning, have you ever seen anything that compared to this?" a reporter put the microphone in front of Gus's face.

He smiled broadly showing his new false teeth. "I've seen fights over slips and boats sinking, but no arsons, and certainly no murders that I can remember."

"How sure are you that this is related to the shop fires?"

"Well, we'll let the Fire Marshall decide that for sure, but it looks suspicious to me."

"Do you fellows agree?" she asked his friends. They nodded in unison. Some stood to give their opinions as I sneaked away, but she ran when she spotted Fire Chief Randy step off of the boat close-by. By now the huge yacht along the bulkhead showed life. The old man could be seen on deck alongside his grandniece. You could see the crew serving their coffee and a tray of something I was sure must be fancier than the doughnuts Gus had on the counter. The girl was talking rapidly to the old man who shook his head negatively. You could see her huffing and then she was over the side of the boat and running up the dock toward the reporter. "Excuse me, Miss." she said actually tapping the girl on the shoulder as she spoke with the fire chief. And then she saw him. Stopped. Turned, stumbled. Gus saw her falling and caught her elbow. "Whoa, girl. You see a ghost?"

"I'm a little dizzy. I must have jumped off the boat too soon after waking. Caffeine went to my head."

"Leonard, get the young lady a water, would you?" The old man watched from the yacht. Sent his mate to fetch her back, but she was not yet ready to go. He held out smelling salts, but she didn't need them. Slapped them from her hand.

"Miss," Marley and I had seen what happened and her curiosity took her over before I could stop her. Dave's face went white.

"Is there something you need to tell us about the fire? It looked to me like you were about to say something to that reporter (who Marley shooed away rather rudely). Spill it. We need all the info we can get here," the fire-woman ordered.

"I just wanted to offer a reward for anyone with information leading to the arrest of the arsonist. My uncle did, rather, but he didn't want me to announce it on television. He is a philanthropist, you know, but he keeps his contributions quiet. He likes it here and wants to help."

"That right? Why would he care about this little

town?"

"His mom was from Royal Oak. Brought him here a lot when he was little and it was kind of run down. He loves how the town turned into such a quaint pretty village. Doesn't want it to go back to that smelly place it was in the 1960's."

"How about that?" Marley looked at Gus. "You need to speak with the sheriff about this."

Erich approached and cut Marley off. "You can come with me, Brooke" he said. She smiled at the handsome P.I. and let him take her by the arm.

The crowd and I watched as Erich put her in his car and had a conversation. The sheriff listened as Marley filled him in on what was said. She found Dave aboard the workboat, consoling Arnie. I had heard him earlier promising to help all he could to get the boat restored. Marley said he had a good crew at his garage. They were handy and a couple had great carpenter skills in addition to being mechanical. Marley was pleased that he made the offer. He seemed to have a good heart. Marley leaned against him without a word and let him finish. The men shook hands.

"That was really nice of you, Hon," she said as they found me. "Thanks," he said watching as the girl from the yacht, Brooke, Erich had called her, exit Erich's Volvo® wagon.

"Arnie's in a bad way. Hasn't been making any money lately as it is. Needs to get this thing ready for dredging."

"I see fresh oysters in our future."

"It's all about food for you, isn't it? Speaking of that I bet Poppi's is open by now. How about we beat the crowd to the coffee?"

"I watched as the girl watched Dave and Marley who paid no attention to all the watching. She, as many were, was hell bent on figuring out who was hurting the town. She grabbed Iris by the hand and we all walked to Poppi's together.

WJX reported live on the Morning Break Show that a waterman was the most recent victim of the St. Michaels Firebug. Angel Mercy looked good on camera except that she wore bright red lipstick at all times. It didn't always seem to stay only on her lips. It was often outside the point where her lips ended and her face began. I watched, coffee in hand, as she told the region that St. Michaels was in the grip of an arrogant arsonist and murderer and that no one was safe.

"It seems he or she feels no one can catch him. He is taunting the residents and local law enforcement with his blatant disregard. Now he has taken on a waterman. A slap in the face to hard working Chesapeake Bay watermen . Who is this devil on the shore?" This is Angel Mercy reporting from St. Michaels Harbor."

They cut her off there, but allowed the tape to run. Just like at home, I am sure that those who had grown up on the Eastern Shore of the Chesapeake Bay knew what she meant. People had their ways of getting justice whether the law thought they did a fine job at catching culprits or not. Drug dealers are found floating face down in the water on occasion.

"You don't mess with a waterman's vessel," Iris said, walking up behind me.

"Sounds like the mountains. Mountain Justice it is called. I always wanted to write a novel with that title, but didn't think I should push my luck."

"Dangerous territory. Speaking of that. Knapps must have refused to go with his mother. I saw Erich just pull him off the street. Should we go rescue him?"

"I think they can handle this. I don't want to interfere. If Knapps has more information or ideas about this he should spill it. He could have gotten really hurt. What if there had been an explosion?"

"His mother will be out of her mind with worry until this thing passes."

I was so tired and needed a few hours rest before starting my day…again. I said as much and headed for home, Hank at my heels.

Iris didn't seem so tired. She was wired, either from the coffee or the incident or both. She joined me and when we got home she paced the kitchen, walked out to the pool, stripped to her under clothes and dove in, taunting me to join her. How great the water felt. She kept it heated at this time of year and in the spring. She had a solar cover and was anal about the care of the pool. She had said that swimming relieved her tensions, kept her in shape, and gave her time to think, to let thoughts bounce through her brain at random. As I dove I saw

Knapps in my mind; a boy. He was so happy with his new job as my writer and sales rep. They say he had been a droopy boy. Now he held his head up, did not slouch so much, kept his hands out of his pockets and his hat out of his eyes. At times he actually removed the ragged cap. Locals had not seen his hair in years, they told me. How I longed to cut it!

I fell onto the comfortable unmade bed that made me dream as soon as I closed my eyes. With Hank curled at my feet, I could not help but sleep. Knapps was a bit older in my dream, was swearing that his mother was innocent. That she worked the night shift lately and could not be the firebug. He demanded to be fed-burgers and fries-as he had been in the questioning room in the county jailhouse for some time.

"Don't you have a clue about who is doing this?" he asked. "I should have been a cop."

Marci Lynn McGuinness

CHAPTER 17

When I woke Erich was sitting on my deck with Hank curled up at his feet sleeping like a baby. He had coffee in a warming thermos and an extra mug waiting for me. I didn't say a word, but went to the bathroom, brushed my teeth and hair, splashed water on my face and went to him. I took his hand, pulled him off of the lounger to me. My loins throbbed with desire. Our eyes locked; I took him to my bed.

I kissed him. He picked me up by the waist and I wrapped my legs around him. His hand cupped my small firm breast. He kissed me slowly, pushing Hank toward the door with his foot. He was wagging his tail and jumping at us. Erich put him out of the room, closed the door, and removed his shirt with one hand, holding me there with the other.

"Oh, God," he moaned as he lowered me onto him.

I was already wet for him. Had been for days. And
we really started to get to know each other. He
lowered me to the bed and licked my fingers one at
a time before pulling my hands above my head,
kissing my neck, my eyes, my earlobes. He stroked
my nipples with his thick tongue. I squirmed with
delight. He kissed my belly, rubbed his one day
growth of face hair on my taut skin. As he kissed
around my hair, I lost control before he ever
touched me. He was so hard now. He licked my
fluid. Kissed my thighs. Massaged my buttocks and
brought me to him, licking, kissing, watching me
moan. He entered me with his tongue, pulled back
and removed his shorts. He stood above me. Stared
at my hair spilled across the pillows, glassy eyes,
arms reaching for him. I could see his heart
pounding with desire. I knew then that he wanted
me to love him, not just physically. I got up and
kissed his mouth, tasting myself on him. He pulled
me close and I climbed him until I could feel his
thick firmness against me. I was so very wet with
desire for him. "Cedar," he moaned as he entered
me, lowering me to the bed. Above me he worked
himself into me, out of me, slowly, repeatedly. I
screamed and he kissed me, entering me. He
throbbed and pulled out. He was purple, in pain
with wanting me. I held him, stroked him. He
groaned like an animal and I pulled away, pushed
him onto his back, straddled his muscular dark hairy
masculinity. When he entered me we came together
within minutes, an explosion that shocked us both. I

never wanted to let him out of me. Kept him in, squeezed my muscles together. He rolled me onto my side. We touched and adored each other. Kissing, holding, trying to catch our breath. "Good morning," he whispered finally.

"That it is," I smiled.

He held me close. "We fit together pretty good," he told me.

"Mmmm," was all I could muster. I was so exhausted, exhilarated, scared, in love.

"Now get dressed. I have a surprise for you. We are taking a day off." He ordered.

He led me to the docks where people came and went in their many capacities. Gus and his cronies watched, discussed the boat fire, shook their heads in disgust, and tried to do what they could to help the forlorn. I understood now why arsonists visited their work. The excitement overwhelmed their senses. The smell lingered much like a wood burning fire in a fireplace. The old charred boat sat smoking before us. Sirens had screamed waking every resident. Dogs had howled and barked. People cried, moaned, whispered, lamented revengeful promises, "If I get hold of the bastard I'll kill him before the law knows what happened."

I could also see why people made their livelihoods fighting fires. But arson, now, that was an art few ever mastered. I have read enough to know that arsonists were often not caught and sentenced. Would there be newspaper articles bearing this arsonist's name? When they died would they still be undiscovered, loved and respected or feared and wondered about? There were many theories which tried to explain what ultimately drove people to strike the first match and continue to do so.

When I was only six years old my neighbor's friend lived with his family-mom, dad, sisters, and brother. They got into plenty of mischief like other kids. But one day he decided that he was going to get rid of the ants that lived in the pine trees surrounding his home. His brother was with him. It had been a dry year. He remembered his mother saying that to him over and over. The ants ran around inside this particular tree trunk, busy with their chores of finding and gathering food. He had sat and watched them with his brother many days that summer. The insects never took naps; busy, busy, carrying food here and there. They ran over each other. There was a huge mass of them. Big fat black ants. It was said that he sometimes caught one and popped it between his fingernails like a flea. Later he said he did it to hear his brother squeal, that he had always felt that his younger brother was a bit of a Momma's boy.

I couldn't quit smiling as Erich jumped aboard a 42 foot Pearson and held out his hand to me. From then on I couldn't quit touching him, either. We motored through the Miles River channel markers which were meant to keep us in deep water, and up into the Wye River where we dropped the anchor. He hugged me tight and went into the galley.

Champagne in one hand and a picnic basket in the

other, he looked like a dream to me. I wondered if he shouldn't be on the job that day. If another fire broke out and we were out courting, what would the sheriff do? Well, I decided, we were not his employees, and I realized Erich was only helping out an old friend. I did not believe the sheriff was paying his going rate. Knew he couldn't be.

"A penny for your thoughts," he whispered kissing the area behind my right ear.

"I am so happy to be here with you," I crooned.

"Me, too. Thought we needed some one-on-one time so to speak."

"You thought right. No guilt then."

"Guilt?"

"What if a fire breaks out today?"

"Then maybe the law will do their job and get this guy," he said. "It's obvious to me and the arsonist that they are afraid-in over their heads, but I have a theory, and we can afford to take a break. It's always good to remove oneself from tense situations in order to let things settle in the mind. Clears thinking. Sometimes a minute detail will come to the forefront of the mind when you least expect it. Plus, I needed to be with you. It's that simple."

"Me, too. This guacamole is delicious."

"Wish I'd made it myself." He sat next to me. Fed me a dipped tortilla chip. Kissed the sides of my mouth, the end of my nose. "Thanks for coming along," he said, looking at me intently.

"What a morning. What possessed you to be waiting

on the deck for me to wake up?"

"Possessed is the word. I couldn't take it anymore."
I leaned into him, practically purred. "Hank really
likes you, but when you tossed him out of the room,
I think you lost points."

"He's a guy. He understands. A toast. May we be
lucky enough to hold onto the lust and love we feel
today."

My eyes popped at the word "love," but I clicked
my glass to his and took a sip, a deep breath, and
closed my eyes for a second.

"A promise. No talk about the arsons today, okay?"

"No problem," I agreed, happy to be playing hooky
with this beautiful, interesting, yummy man.

I had sailed a little on Deep Creek Lake in Garrett
County, but really had no experience with it other
than going along for the ride. After we made love
again and again, ate the brie and Gala apples, and
emptied the champagne, he began teaching me the
basics of sailing. I took the wheel. "Whose boat is
this?" I asked.

"It's mine. I spend a lot of time on it, although I
have the brownstone in Baltimore. I had a buddy of
mine bring it over from the inner harbor."

"So you've been plotting on me then?"

"You bet. Now don't turn the wheel. This isn't a
car. Just move it slightly. Keep your eyes on that
island up ahead and steer toward it. I'll handle the
winches. Watch the depth finder, too. This Bay is a
shallow mother."

"Eye Eye, Captain." I saluted.

CHAPTER 18

When Erich and I walked through the police station door we could see the sheriff was pacing his office. The District Attorney was clearly reminding him of his incompetence, threatening to turn this over to the state troopers. "This has gone on too long, sheriff. You don't seem to be making one bit of progress. When will we see an arrest?"

"Very soon. I can't just go out and arrest people on flimsy evidence. I don't care who is on the job, there is little evidence to be had. Your people know this as well as I do."

"No witnesses?"

"Plenty of maybes. Nothing concrete, but I am gaining."

"I know you are working with your hotshot friend. Why the hell hasn't he nailed someone? Someone had to see the old man get hit."

"Give us time, sir."

"Why, to wait for the next fire? This is a tiny village. How difficult could it be to find a firebug amongst you?"

"I am working on a couple leads and if you'll excuse me, I'll get this settled much faster."

District Attorney Laser let out a sigh. "I'm giving this two more days, then I am bringing in the troops. We can not be made a mockery just because we are Eastern Shore boys."

"Yes, sir. State boys have no more than we do."

As Laser exited he paused at the sight of us. We were a bit rumpled, I'd imagine. He just nodded and went outside.

"Where the hell have you been?" the sheriff insisted. "I'm praying that you have been on the trail of this criminal." He placed his hat upon his balding head and started out the door to make his rounds as his young deputy came rushing through and asked to see him in his office.

"I may have an idea about this, sir. I can't tell you how often I see this guy loading up his gas can. He has always given me the creeps."

"Who? What do we have that says we can bring him in for questioning?

"I saw him last night at the town meeting with his wife. He watched everyone like they were the enemy. I know you can't arrest people for their attitude, but maybe I can question him without bringing him in. Do a stop-by."

"You have yet to tell me who this is," the sheriff was now scratching his belly.

"Dave that's married to Marley, that firewoman," he tried to whisper.

"That so? Why do you think he is suspect? He owns the lot and sells those ATVs. He has always had a can or two with him."

"That's right, but he just acts guilty to me."

"You may certainly keep an eye on him, but don't go off half cocked on a hunch,. There is nothing that says this has anything to do with Dave. Marley will know his alibi. Leave that to me."

Knapps felt like they thought he was the firebug/murderer since he found Mr. Faith, the boat burnt, and he saw someone burn Iris' place. "When you can't find the real bad guy, blame a kid," he told me. We were finishing up the latest newspaper. "How about this, 'St. Michaels Fire Bug still Bugs St. Michaels'?"

"I think he's doing more than bugging us. Iris and many shop owners are literally ready to lynch this guy, and by the way, you were on the water when Agnes died."

"That's right," he let out a breath, but it hasn't been that long ago since the last hanging."

"Was it done by the courts?"

"Nah, a mob. I wrote a paper about it senior year. He was kind of slow. Raped his neighbor. She was a beauty, too. I can see how it happened. She was nice to him. Felt sorry for him probably. Thought he was harmless and she was doing a good thing cause no one else paid him any mind. He worked on her father's tomato farm."

I pictured this in my mind as Knapps told the tale. "He was caught pretty quick cause she told her mom what happened. But he got away when the sheriff was trying to put him in his cell after the first day of the trial. The courtyard in Easton was full of angry people. They were pushing to get at him when the sheriff was walking him through his office. He let go for just a minute and the mob shoved him aside. The guy went out an office window and ran like hell with cuffs on his hands."

"Oh my God! When was this?"

"It was 1920 or so. Anyway, no one saw him go cause the sheriff was trying to control the crowd. He was my great grandfather, the sheriff, I mean. Anyway, he ran and the mob got organized and got dogs and they all went hunting him. It took a couple days. Can you believe that? But he was found starving in an old shed in Whitman. They brought him back for another trial which took forever cause a city lawyer took over and postponed everything a couple times. People were pissed. Oh, excuse my language, but you can imagine. Finally they charged him with first degree rape and sentenced him to thirty years. That wasn't good enough for the local farmers. They waited until the sheriff was going to move him and put hoods over their heads. Stopped the sheriff. Took the guy. Hung him in the barn where he raped the girl."

"Is this true?"

"It's a story I've heard all my life."

"Did they arrest these guys?"

"No one was charged. The sheriff must have been paid off or threatened. I don't know, but from what I read he was pretty tough in his own right. Maybe he wanted him hung, too."

"Yeah, maybe," I sighed, stretched. "You think that could happen today?"

"Nothing would surprise me, but these people here today are mostly imports. They haven't got the passion. They're old!"

I turned back to the computer screen. Iris interrupted just then with a bottle of wine. "Hey guys, I got my insurance check. Paying those high premiums has paid off!" she poured three glasses and made a toast. "May the arsonist get burnt in the next fire!"

Knapps and I looked at each other with raised eyebrows. Not everyone was old and passionless.

Marci Lynn McGuinness

CHAPTER 19

Erich felt he was onto something. It had been edging into his mind for some time. After two decades of P.I. work, a guy knew to listen to his gut, he confided in me. Instinct told him that this was not your everyday arsonist spree and that Dave was not their man. He had been with Marley or had alibis for all the fires, so even questioning him was a waste of time. So, who had Knapps really seen? Years ago someone was burning shops in Ellicott City near Baltimore. The historical district was just being revamped, and he had gone to several meetings about the progress. Huge grants and loans were at stake to remodel the many stone and brick century old structures then standing vacant on Main Street. Ellicott City was by no means the bustling burgh it is today, but was obviously up and coming. Many long time residents were disgruntled, not all, but enough to get his curiosity up. The first fire looked like an accident, so did the second and third, but he knew coincidences like that don't often happen. Not in the real world. Humans cause harm more often than not. Unhappy people bring on most of the sadness and violence in the world. That has been his experience, and he has seen plenty.

The Mayor of Ellicott City was beside himself. On one hand he had worked days and nights for years to get to the place where the state agreed that his town was where the money should go. The evening he cut the first ribbon on the first building to be renovated, it burnt. A gas fire. Old newspapers. Sounded too familiar. A man died at the scene supposedly setting the fourth fire. Heart attack. Erich never believed this was the arsonist. Felt for sure he knew who it was, but the local law was so intent on closing the case that it was dropped. He watched the guy he felt was responsible for several more years. No more fires were set. He got away with it and went on with his life. Of course, the town was redone and new shops and restaurants draw tourists and more residents. This is what, he believed, the firebug was trying to put a stop to. Didn't work. A man lost his life, and an arsonist still lived among the elite of the town.

Often in life he just had to take what he could get from a case and move on. He earned his keep. Was hired by the Mercantile Bank to see that they were not next. They weren't. Although the police closed the case, his buddy on the force let him know that they knew Erich was right. They couldn't prove it and would watch the guy he suspected the rest of his life. People stopped living in fear. That is what was necessary for a town to get on with living.

I met Marley and Iris after an early delivery of my newspaper. Knapps would go to Tilghman with the remainder later. He was a big help and I was thrilled that he was coming into his own so quickly. He wrote a story on the "Peninsula People" for this issue. An esoteric look at locals and how they look at imported people. It was insightful, funny, and brought out talents even he never realized he had. I was thinking of asking him to help write the book on the arsonist. I had it started, but his input would make it something that would really sell. At least, I believed it would. We'd publish it ourselves. What an array of characters, I was thinking, as I approached the girls. They waited on the bench in front of the Post Office, chatting animatedly.

"Hey, Lois Lane," Marley greeted me waving a strong arm.

I laughed. "We walking to this auction?"

"No, we need to haul away our goods! It's a gorgeous day. Let's enjoy it, okay?" Iris asked.

"Yeah, lets," Marley agreed. She was looking great, in love. Life was good. And then we saw them. At first we didn't realize they were together. The pretty girl from the big yacht was sitting on a scooter. They got in Dave's car together behind the Christmas Shoppe. No one saw them but us. Marley breathed deeply. Told us there was a simple reason.

She wanted to buy a car. Rent a car. Trade in her
scooter. He had always been good to her and
faithful and St. Michaels was not a place where
affairs went on unnoticed. He was not that dumb.
She was sure of that. And he loved her, she knew in
her gut. "Let's go. I am not spying on my husband."
"Wow! Look at all of those cars," I screeched as we
pulled up to the auction site. The whole town was
there it seemed. They say that when Mr. Meton died
he did not leave a will. His family had been fighting
over his money for years so he just let things go. He
had retired here ten years before. Always said they
were just waiting for him to kick the bucket. Now
he did and they were selling everything he owned.
We girls meant to find a few interesting bargains.
We walked around the crowd to see what we could
see and to get our auction numbers.
We tried to forget what we saw. They would meet
for lunch as planned and he would tell her about his
morning, she insisted. She put on a smile, got her
number and told them she would soon own the
maple mantle that leaned against the front porch.
You could tell her mind wondered as the bidding
began. We would be there a while. All the small
stuff would go first. Iris bought some great jewelry.
I bought myself an oak desk to die for. More
drawers than anyone had ever seen before. I
planned on renting an office and setting up a
newspaper office. We couldn't work in my bedroom
forever. I could store the desk in the big shed
behind the house in the meantime. I also bought

antique 4-drawer wooden file cabinets.
Then the fire whistle blew.

The Penny Cabin Inn has lived an interesting life. It
was first built as a cabin, then was turned into the
hot spot of the town where bands played and
crowds gathered for fun and frolic. Today many
locals had mixed feelings about the inn, but it was
top-notch and attracted high-powered political
meetings and film crews for hit movies. The food
was good, but there were so many top notch eateries
on the Eastern Shore, competition was fierce.
Today smoke billowed from what looked like one
of the new hotel buildings. The construction crew
was putting it out the fire already, but the bright
white "cabin" that held 33 rooms would be a wash.
Black smoke filled the sky while firemen figured
out where to go.
I saw Erich go in. The construction crew hadn't
seen anything out of the ordinary, but the unfinished
rooms had been sprinkled with gas. Everyone
smelled it. Did this place not have security guards?
Just as the thought crossed my mind, one
approached him.
"I'll lose my job over this," he whined to Erich.
"Did you see anyone this morning? Had to be set
just before these guys got here."
"Yeah, I guess so. No. Nothing unusual, I'd think,"
the security guard stated.
"The English, proper under pressure," I thought.

We could see Randy driving the loud fire-truck
coming up the brick lane and heading our way.
"We must stop meeting like this," Erich said
hugging me and kissing the top of my head. I
blushed, but Marley was too busy to comment. Iris
just stared. Her shop was starting to be rebuilt just
across the street. These people - the visitors who
stayed at the inn - spent big money on picnics to
take out on the charter boats working from this
dock. Where would this end?

Erich watched the crowd. He turned 180 degrees
until he saw something in the woods between the
museum and the new buildings. He excused
himself, got in his car as if leaving and headed up
the other side road.

At least the fire kept Marley's mind off of seeing
her husband in what looked like an intimate
conversation with the girl Erich had called Brooke.
I'd bet she would like to have hold of the arsonist
right now. She'd pity him…after choking him.

"Marley, we need you over here!" I heard Randy
call to her.

The flames shot out of the new roof. I could see the
place was a loss no matter how fast she moved, but
she moved quickly none-the-less. It was amazing
what a crowd fires attracted. Of course, the inn was
pretty full in September. Weddings and conferences
went on all year. The media, too, amazed me that
they arrived so quickly. I carried a compact digital
camera in my bag. This fire would piss off the

owners, I knew. They would not take this lightly.
Oh, no, this was no independent shop on the Eastern
Shore struggling for that tourist dollar. It would be
interesting, I thought, as they hosed the roof, to see
who they brought in to investigate in this podunk
town now. Very interesting.

I did not believe Dave was cheating on Marley, but
what was he up to? We couldn't be the only ones in
this nosy town who saw them together. Where did
they go? That was the question. Where was he and
what the hell was he doing while his wife fought
this fire and risked her life? She didn't seem to be a
crier by nature, but today I bet, she fought back the
tears. Could blame them on the smoke if anyone
saw her red eyes, though.

As things got under control Randy came to us
mumbling. "This has got to stop, Iris, damn! This
job used to be fun!"

"Someone's having fun. I wish I knew who the hell
it was," Iris patted his shoulder.

Randy looked to the sky. "At least no one got hurt,"
he said slumping his back and walking way.

We watched as the sheriff had his deputies tape the
area off. That was becoming a commonplace scene,
I realized. Were they starting to accept the fires?
People did not seem very angry here today. They all
seemed so quiet.

"Was that a shot?" I yelled to Iris who stood a good
50 yards away, close to the wooded area between
the inn and the Chesapeake Bay Maritime Museum.
Iris pointed to the woods. I ran in that direction with

my camera. Marley ran, too. Who knew what was going on? Maybe it was just a duck hunter in the wrong area.

We all stopped as we watched Erich put an old man up against a tree. He must have shot in the air when he tried to get on the scooter and get away. A scooter lay on its side. Was that decrepit old man their arsonist? Could we have been fooled by this man who no one ever noticed? We didn't believe what we were seeing…for the second time that day.

"You smell like gas."

"I just cut my grass this morning."

Erich was visibly irritated by now. Why did he think this old fart was the guy? Sure he was lurking in the woods, but being weird is no crime.

"Mr. Flynn. Your behavior is quite suspicious. You have been to every fire. You blatantly carry that gas can with you as if showing off. You've been seen trying doors of other businesses when they aren't open."

"I do handiwork. Paint. Stuff like that in lots of places around town. I'm retired, bored. I'm not your man."

"We'd like to be sure about that. This is the sixth fire in two months. People are not going to be very kind when you walk down the streets knowing we suspect you."

"I don't care what people think."

"Where were you when Lumpy's burnt?"

"In bed."

"We'll need to speak to your wife."

Just then his wife walked up. She was shaking. She looked up at them with anxious eyes. I thought she was the sweetest old lady I had ever seen. Motherly looking. Bet she baked muffins and cookies. Took good care of her husband.

"Ma'am, can you tell me where your husband was during all the fires? Do you know?"

"Of course. I always know where he is. He is a very routine person. He spends his morning reading several newspapers. Doesn't sleep well so he's up very early. Goes out and gets them at the stands in front of the Post Office. He reads and drinks coffee, then does chores - yard work. He likes to work in the flower and vegetable garden. Today was no different. At times he paints for shop owners."

Smug, I thought, or was she just trying not to cry? I wasn't sure.

"Do you realize why he is here?

"You can't think my Andy is your firebug! That's preposterous. He is just not the kind of man who takes risks. Never has been. What is your evidence? What is his motive? He listens to that police radio of his and goes to all the fires and accidents. He is bored."

"He's been seen messing about the burnt buildings both before and after the fires. We are not sure about the why. Arsonists don't always have a logical reason, but boredom is the norm."

"Well, this town is filled with bored retired people. Any one of them could be doing it."

Erich couldn't help but laugh about that. It was true enough. He knew he would have to let him go.

"Does Andy smoke?"

"A pipe," she huffed. "That illegal, too? I am so embarrassed. The ladies I play bridge with will be appalled."

"Yes, Ma'am. I want you to keep a good eye on your husband. If I catch him lurking around any of the fire sites again, I'm pulling him for more than questioning."

"I always know where my husband is."

The sheriff stepped up. "And Justine's is just behind your home. Where were you then?"

"Home alone eating lunch until I smelled smoke."

"Not an alibi, is it? We will be watching you. You can go home now, but don't leave town without my knowledge."

His wife took his arm without a word . We watched them hobble to her car talking in very low voices. For some reason, I did not think he was the one. It was a gut feeling, and I always follow my instincts. Sure, he looks guilty. Would be easy to hang this on him. Everyone would feel better. BUT, would the fires stop, and if they did, would the real arsonist/murderer get off Scott free? Would we be living with him everyday? Speaking to him at the Post Office? Nodding hello at the Acme? See him walking his dog and think nothing of it?

I needed to ponder these thoughts before sitting down to write. I ran faster and Hank smiled as he ran with me. I loved that dog smile. It said, "You're

my Mom and you are the best person on the earth."
So he is naive, what of it? I knew Erich had good
instincts, and I wasn't convinced he felt the old guy
was the culprit. I wondered what it was he was
thinking. It was very confusing. I tried to stop
thinking and let the air clear my mind so I could see
reality.

A blue pick-up truck slowed beside me. "Hey, girl,"
Gus yelled. "Need a ride?"

"Hi Gus! I've never seen you away from your
marina. You sure it won't drop into the harbor with
you away?"

He laughed at that. "I have help once in a while. Get
in."

I tried to catch my breath and tell him that I
preferred to run when the passenger door flung
open. "Geez, you are a gentleman," I smiled closing
it. "But I am going to finish this run."

"Suit yourself," he said and pulled away, turning
around in the driveway of the nature preserve.

I wondered where he had been going. Maybe he
was just riding around watching. Many were. At
home, my uncle spent all his free time doing just
that. He knew what everyone was doing. He never
really had a destination, just watching over his
kingdom, he'd tell you if you asked. I used to stand
in the middle of the road in front of my store if I
needed him, knowing he would be around soon.
Going looking for him was fruitless. He could be
anywhere, but I knew he'd drive by and see that all
was well on my home front at least twelve times a

day. Ohiopyle's own crime watch. St. Michaels could use him right now. This would be solved. They happened more than people realized, unsolved crimes. Police were stumped more than they solved this type of thing. It must be a mighty frustrating business. Erich was called in to solve things. He is the expert, so why was the culprit still terrorizing them? Why didn't he just snatch the guy up? No evidence. No one seems to be coming forth with information except for Knapps, even with the award I posted in my paper. I've had calls, but nothing substantial. Sure Millie Day saw her neighbor leave with a gas can. There were gas cans in every truck and boat on the shore. Proved nothing and made it next to impossible to pinpoint the bad guy. He must have been planning this a while. Realized how easy it would be to do it this way. Must be laughing like hell.

I was out of breath and my mind whirred instead of cleared as I headed upstairs to check my messages. I rewound and listened again. It was a faint voice. Were they whispering or what? Turning the volume up as high as it would go I thought they said, "You have the wrong guy."

"Was that a woman or man? Damn!" I cursed, stripping out of my running clothes and stepping into a hot shower. "You've got the wrong guy. Figures, but we have no guy. How odd!"

The next day Marley told us about Dave.

"That's not your happy to see me face, Hon," he

smirked.

"I saw you with that woman from the yacht."

"Oh, she is here with her family. Is obsessed because I rejected her years ago. She hired a Private Detective to find me once!"

"What's she want from you now? What does she think you owe her?"

"She is rich and spoiled and angry. Thinks she loves me, hates me. I don't even owe her an explanation. She knows why I had to go. Her temper, her money, she wielded them like a sword whenever the desire possessed her. It was more than I could stomach. At first she entertained me, but she wore me down. Made me feel used, overpowered. Her family's money lorded over me. I could never be a man in my own home as long as I was with her.

One night she took a couple sleeping pills and I just walked out. Took a cab to the airport. Traveled for a few months with the cash I had been saving. One day in the Florida Keys a fishing buddy asked if I'd like to crew a boat with him. They were moving it north to the Chesapeake Bay for the summer season. I always wanted to see the Bay. When we landed on Tilghman Island, I knew it was as good a place to hide as any. I really feared her wrath. She thought she owned me. I wanted to be free of her. I have been free for several years. I love my wife, my home, my life, and business. Enjoy the slow pace and great eats of the Eastern Shore.

She stared at him. "You should have told me about this long ago. Where did you leave things with her?"

"I told her I won't play her game and she needed to get on with her life."

"What we had was over years ago. Why should I hide? I've nothing to hide. I told her I adore and love my wife and she needs to go home."

He whirled her around and kissed her passionately.

"So that is it?" Iris asked her friend.

"I have a bad feeling about her, but it is up to Dave to handle this."

"Penny for your thoughts," Iris said to me.

"I was just thinking about some fires in Pennsylvania. Someone burnt a bunch of libraries. It went on for months and then just stopped. They never caught the guy."

"Ye of little faith," Marley mused, touching my shoulder. Hank jumped at her to get her attention so she bent to pet the funny hound.

"It just seems so crazy. That old man didn't do all this, did he?" Iris asked.

"I can't really say. I doubt it," Marley sighed.

He pulled in the dock lines so I could step on deck. Hank ran to the bow looking out into the river, sniffing those fishy smells he so adored. Erich took me in his arms and just let me mold into the form of his body. We went below in silence, undressed each other, looked into each other's eyes for a long moment. He was on his knees in a flash, taking my wetness into his mouth. When I caught my breath, I pulled him to me wrapping my legs around his waist while he stood thrusting himself into me. In and out, in and out, slowly, gradually more powerfully until I screamed into his shoulder, going blind with the ecstasy of coming together.

He grinned, kissing me on the neck, the lips, the eyes, reached into the small frig and took out two bottles of water, whipping off the lids and tossing them into a bucket. Hank watched as he poured a bit into a bowl for him.

"Maybe it's time we worked together," he said.

"Define work," I smiled.

He laughed. I sat on his lap, water bottle turned up.

"I have been thinking."

Knapps and I looked over the ground floor of the newly remodeled shop at 202 Talbot Street. The upstairs was still being refurbished. It was cute. The clapboard building was painted a bright yellow with muted navy shutters. The front windows were beveled glass, giving off a lot of light. Hardwood floors, a small kitchen and restroom with shower. I envisioned Knapps and myself hard at work in the front room. The two back rooms would be used for a private office with files and my desk. The other would be a parlor. It had a tiny courtyard with no grass, but a covered porch held a swing that had just been sanded and repainted. It gleamed in the sunlight. Ground ivy, flowering shrubs, and exotic flowers made the back yard into a haven where a writer could think.

Stairs led up to the top floor. The owner, Jacob

Knots, was finishing the dry wall. Dust rolled out of the back door as I tried to get his attention. "I'll take it," I yelled in the door, covering my mouth, nose, and eyes.

"You sure? It could be burnt down before you know it the way things are going."

"I thought of that, but I am not one to let anyone stop me from doing what I need to do," I said, ascending the steps.

"Me neither. I like that." He smiled showing a missing front tooth."

We shook on the deal as I handed him a deposit check and signed lease."

. "I'll move my things in as soon as you think it will be ready for business."

"I'll be done making a lot of noise around here in two days. Then it's just painting and clean-up. The hard work is over."

"Sounds good to me," I grinned and went downstairs. Knapps stood in the doorway looking at the back yard.

"Wow. This is cool. Who knew this was here?"

"A real perk, huh? Inspiring place to write."

"Thanks, Cedar. Thanks for talking to me that first morning and everything since."

"You looked harmless to me."

He physically flinched. Looked like he got a chill up his spine or saw a ghost. Erich walked up behind him. "This is you, Cedar. Fits you to a tee."

"Thanks."

Knapps backed into the office area while Erich

came to me. He was not about to watch us smooch. I watched him as he looked around. I supposed he imagined himself writing in the window. Having people see him, Knapps Reckon, trusted journalist. I looked into Erich's gorgeous green eyes. We had known each other such a short time, and the chemistry was powerful. I wanted him to be someone I could trust with all my information. My conscience told me I must spill now. So I did. "I had a phone call," I started. He froze, his hands around my back loosened slightly. "A man said that we didn't have the right person." I handed him the tape. A copy, of course.

He pulled his recorder from his pocket and slapped it in. We listened. "I know that voice. They are trying to deepen it, but I know that voice." He paced. I loved the way the dent between his eyebrows deepened as he pondered. My sailor, my P.I., I thought. I also thought he may be too good to be true. Hoped I would some day be able to set myself free in that arena, and believe fully in love. He stood in the doorway watching the street. People came in and out of the Post Office, the Bank, the shops. I rubbed his shoulders from behind, laid my cheek on his firm back, his denim shirt for a second. Wondered where Knapps got to.

"What else do you know that I should know, Cedar? You have to trust me on this. If I don't have all the clues, the puzzle can't come together, and this town can't get on with the lifestyle it has grown so accustomed to. You'll never be able to move into this office. This guy will burn you out because of the articles you write."

"I thought about that. There may be one other thing." It set my spine into goose bumps although I can't believe what I'm thinking. 'I was running the other day and Gus stopped to ask if I needed a ride. I'm not sure why that made me nervous. He seemed different away from the dock. I felt like he wanted something from me. I ran home, but he turned the truck around. Didn't continue along the road as if he just happened on me, you know? He turned his truck around and passed me slowly again. I can tell you it gave me the creeps. I visit him at the bench sometimes. Him and his friends. We talk. I have always felt comfortable doing that. He encouraged me to start the paper when I first got here. What do you make of it?"

"I think you should not be going anywhere alone until this thing is settled. I am going to need to be working night and day. Can you be with me, help me if I need it? Back off if I need it? Do what I say?"

"I've never been very obedient, but I see what you mean. I'd like to work with you on this. It'll help the town and advertisers will flock through this door."

"Always the business woman. But I need you safe, and you seem to be gathering evidence for some reason. All these people have lived here forever and they can't tell me a thing. They watch and see nothing. You take a walk and get hassled, then get home to a recorded message. Who is that dumb to leave a recorded message?"

"Lots of people," I said snuggling up to him.

The town looked like so much char. Although crews worked diligently to remove the damaged buildings and begin new construction, St. Michaels gave one the feeling that the devil was winning. Erich couldn't take it anymore. He began being gruff with just about everyone. He wanted someone to let down their guard. He had his intuitions, but needed to set someone up to fall into a trap so he could settle this dilemma.

There were two men he suspected could be burning the town. Neither one felt right to him, though. We watched as the town played out its day. Sat on the Post Office bench for hours, speaking to everyone who entered and exited and passed by. After hundreds of conversations and sensations, we walked to his boat. Randy came tumbling off his boat not three slips away. He looked like hell-3 day beard, unbathed, dark circles under the eyes, beer in hand. Dusk was upon us. He didn't notice us and we watched the fire chief rub his face with both hands. It didn't help. Gus waved to both us, shaking his head. Gus saw all. Many people in this town did, so why didn't they see the arsonist? Didn't add up. Someone knew more than they were giving up, but why? Why would anyone want this for this lovely village? It was turning into a sight. Not a tourist site, but an unsightly sight. And the smell that hit you when you got just past Dave's car lot was old burnt wood. Not like in a fireplace, either. Forget that cozy picture. This turned the stomach, made it roll.

People seemed resilient. They were getting on with their lives. Erich sat on deck with a cold beer. I knew he was thinking about the night that would come in short order. We had talked with many that day. Conversations sifted through my organized mind and I am sure, his.

"Cedar, you are a writer, a business woman, and have an imaginative mind. People seem to be drawn to you, and I am more than most, I admit." He grinned. "You also have investigative instincts. I feel the arsonist is going to come after you next. Those articles must be spooking him and now that you are moved into the office on Talbot Street, well, how could he resist the temptation to put you in your place? I am asking you for your own safety to please stay close to me."

I looked at him and my heart almost burst as I saw Randy out of the corner of my eye looking to the sky.

Iris had been at loose ends since her shop burnt. She was used to working hard. Her customers saw to that. And she needed them more than she knew. Not just for a livelihood, either. To stay focused. To stay sane. It wasn't that she was poor without the store. She had confided that her savings had grown and her investments were sound. The life insurance money she collected after her husband's death was still untouched. But she recently realized she needed stimulation, and not just sex. Her mind needed to be occupied. She was a business woman needing to get down to business. She had finally found a good crew who threw her shack up in record time. Now the plumbers were giving her fits, and she was in no mood. The place looked good. And she was able to add a small café to its character. She had had a few tables inside and out, but had them build a new counter where you could eat or have a latte. Erich and I pulled up a stool. The kitchen was first class, much to cook Riley's joy. He was already getting down to making oyster stew.

"Miss Iris, you think we should order supplies, just to have them ready to ship here in case these guys actually ever get us some water in here?

"Might be a good idea to at least put together an opening order and get these shelves stocked. We must get ready and get back to work. Can't use bottled water forever."

"I agree, Miss Iris. My wife wants me outa that house quick as she can get me out."

We all laughed at that. Iris wanted out of the house, too. Stir crazy was not her cup of tea. Her cell phone rang. The electrician would be late. Looking out into the street we could see that the oyster festival was packing them in at the Chesapeake Bay Maritime Museum. This was usually one of her biggest weekends for the entire year. It obviously and rightly irked her. She had hoped to show off her new place this weekend.

"Welcome," Iris said as Randy stood in the doorway.

He honestly looked like a starved cat. "You gonna get this place open while we still have oysters?"

"Yes, that I promise."

"I am so tired of wondering around in a daze. I just can't believe Agnes is gone for good."

"It's not easy, I know," she said leading him to a stool next to us.

He looked around the place. "I'm ready to see this place jumping again. I hate getting my lottery tickets at the convenience store. They are awful slow there, and they act like they don't know you."

"Does anyone really know anyone?" she looked him over.

"Some do," he mumbled.

He was having no fun. The fires even started boring him. It's just this town, he thought. It's for retired people, and I am not the kind of person who should have retired. Sure, the odd jobs helped, but they did not keep a man busy enough. His mind wandered. He rarely slept. "You coming to bed?" Martha called from the bathroom as she prepared for her long night's rest. It amazed him that she could just fall to sleep each and every night of her life at the same time and never wake up for at least eight hours. He hadn't even been able to do that as a child. He wandered the streets at night even then. It was startling what one could learn about a town and its people in the wee hours. He could be a writer or a detective like that new couple in town. Some thought he was off his rocker, he realized. There is always someone in every small town who is misunderstood, thus pegged as odd. He felt that he was that person in St. Michaels. He didn't want friends. Never really did through life. Didn't see the point, really. Friends would want to call him on the phone and borrow his tools. Never!

A loner, that's what Martha called him. It doesn't make me a bad person, he always told her. She knew him well. She was his one and only friend. And a loyal friend. It amazed him how she loved him all these years when no one had ever considered him the least bit loveable. His own parents found him a bit stand-offish. That's the word they used to describe him when they thought he wasn't listening. "George is a bit standoffish. Don't pay any attention. He doesn't mean to be rude. It is just his way."

He put his cap upon his head and stepped out into the night air. Martha was already snoring loud enough to shake the walls. He stretched his long bony but muscled arms above his head. Sure, he knew he was being watched. It was the only interesting thing happening in his life, so he would go with it. Watch me walk around the town. Watch me read the paper. I hope it all gives them a thrill. Just because he was a bit independent didn't make him a bad guy, either. Everyone couldn't be preppies, club members or watermen. God made him different and he felt blessed in that way. Self contained, Martha said. She didn't mind. When they were younger and her friends complained to her about their carousing drinking husbands who paid more attention to football and their friends than to their wives and families, she would say that I always came home to her. That I was a gentleman. That I spent my time taking her to dinner, watching television with her, reading in the next chair. She felt that she was lucky. And so did her lady friends. Martha was always smiling. Not so for most women, he knew. He watched the way "normal" men treated their wives. It was shameless. He loved Martha. She was his life. He could not live without her, he knew. He would kill himself if she was ever to die before him. He had had true love for over fifty years and nothing he could experience after her passing would compare. He lifted his head to see a man in dark clothes running across the street with a gas can. Ah, now. It does pay to be a night owl.

Clear skies topped the day. I wanted to get out there. I promised to work the lunch shift, but couldn't manage to concentrate on the busy crowd. I wanted to set up my new office. Erich filled my thoughts, too. Made it difficult to concentrate on white wine and cold draft beer.

"You're that girl I keep seeing with Erich." I turned to see the girl from the yacht, pretty, cocky, tan.

"Like a drink with that menu?" I smiled cautiously.

"He is one hunk of a man, that one." The woman licked her lips and laughed. I looked at her until she lowered her eyes to the menu. Women like that never unnerved me. I found her pitiful. Always trying to cause trouble, high school mentality. Never liked high school. Never could tolerate ignorance, either. I walked away and served a few waitresses and waiters. They were fun people, the staff at Town Dock. Always friendly. Always a joke. Interested in what I was doing. I never felt on the defense with them, as I did immediately with this particular customer. But I smiled. Oh yes, I smiled and took the order for her calamari salad. The lady's eyes darted about. Was she waiting for someone or just looking for her next prey? Kent sat down two stools away from her and ordered his usual red wine. He munched on the dish of mixed nuts, minding his own business. Often, he pulled me into interesting conversations about my life and his. He was about to retire and move he and his writer wife to Delaware where they would be free from taxes. Where they could afford a very nice house after selling their over priced home in St. Michaels. They had family there and would enjoy being closer to the water. He and Doc were my favorite customers, but they were rarely there at the same time. Doc came in around 6 P.M. after his work out at the gym. The man was well into his 70's--78, I think, but he still ran his business full time, worked out, and drank a couple scotches before heading for home most evenings.

Jerry came hustling through the swinging kitchen doors with a tray full of entrees on her shoulder. The lady at the bar looked her up and down. I thought she had probably never worked a job in her life. Just worked people. I removed the empty salad dish in front of her and slid the bill in its place without offering her another drink or dessert. She sat there with her mouth open. I ignored her.

Erich walked in just then and took the seat at the end of the bar. I poured him an iced tea and kissed him on the lips. The girl moved over next to him as I turned to mix a few drinks for the staff. When I turned back around he was pushing her off of him. His hands were around both of her wrists, warning her to behave with a smile on his face. She kissed his cheek, gave me a smirk, threw a twenty on the bar, and wiggled her butt on the way out the door. I looked at Erich. "An old client," he said. "Likes trouble."

"And men. She mentioned you when she came in."

"More money than is safe to have. She's not a very smart girl. That doesn't help. I want you to come with me when you get out of here. Need you to ask someone a question. I'll stay in the background and wait."

"Why do I feel like bait all of a sudden."

"Not bait. An investigative reporter. Just one question in particular I want you to ask...as if it just occurred to you."

"What's it worth to you?"

"Plenty."

CHAPTER 20

Erich stepped through the door first and the sheriff jumped, jolted from his thinking. I was right behind him. He relayed that he had questioned Dave and felt he was not their man. You could see that he felt defeated.

"I have never had an original thought and know I never will." Looking at us, he scratched his belly. "It is obvious you two are up to something, but what? Is there news? Something you need to share with me?"

"Yes, we are going to set a trap," Erich said.

I smiled. "I am leasing the new office space from Mr. Knots. We feel that we can lore the culprit to try to burn me out with a headline that is sure to upset him. What do you think?"

"Sounds dangerous, but I know we can pull it off if we have the place watched all day and night. I like it. Does Jacob know and approve?"

"Not yet, but he is very anxious to get this guy, too. He doesn't want all his hard work burnt to the ground as soon as it is ready to bring in income."

"I see what you mean. Cedar, you don't have to be the sitting duck here, you know. You must think St. Michaels is a crazy place to have moved to. Nothing has been at its usual slow pace since you rode into town."

"I'm ready if we are all in agreement," I said. "I'd like to get my business going without this hanging over us."

Iris and I were eating when Marley burst through the screen door, letting it slap shut behind her with a final bang. Ralph and Hank came running, barking and jumping, rubbing against her for affection.

"Let her in the door, guys," Iris said looking at her friend, her eyebrows coming together. "Marley, you look like hell."

"I oughta."

She led her to a chair at the table and automatically poured her a glass of merlot. "Catch your breath and sip this, girl. Looks like we need to talk."

Marley obeyed. Tried to get her breathing back to normal. Dark damp hair fell into her face as she looked into the wine for answers. Iris pulled a chair close in front of her dear friend. "Now spill," she said quietly, pushing the hair from her eyes.

"Between the fires, murders, and this stalker woman I am losing my mind," she wailed.

"What's going on now?" I asked petting the dogs.

"You know anything new about that dark haired girl running around here on a scooter?"

"Yeah, she was a client of Erich's. Came in taunting me about him today. He set her straight, though, when he came in."

"Erich sent her here? Oh, I'll bet he didn't know who I married when he gave her the information," Marley spit.

Pouring wine for all three of us while we hashed things out, she closed the door and locked it. "Let's go into the den where we can talk privately. These kitchen windows give us away out here."

We followed her. Marley grabbed the bottle off the kitchen counter. We sat in cushy chairs facing one another. Books filled shelves from floor to ceiling, covering three walls. I had never seen this room and wondered how I had missed it.

"It was my husband's hideaway from the world," she explained as she watched me look around at the very nautical décor. The fourth wall was covered with photographs of him with fish, crabs, happy customers, Iris.

"I have never had the heart to change things. It makes me feel close to him. He was a good man." She caught herself and looked at Marley.

"Yeah, he was the best," Marley affirmed. "No two like him unfortunately. What did Erich tell you about this woman?" she demanded facing me.

"He wouldn't divulge because of her client status, but Knapps can dig around for you I'll bet. No one would suspect him.

"He likes older women," Iris offered. She and Marley laughed. "Oh, Cedar, You know he has a crush on you."

"Not like that!"

"Whatever you say, but I don't think he likes sharing you with Erich," Marley put in.

I just smiled at that. What were they to do for Marley? This would be tough for her new friend. I could see how in love she was from the start. Think he is, too, but he also hid his past.

Changing the subject I asked, "Is this woman here to sleep with all the men in town? Her fire needs put out." On that we all agreed.

At the next town meeting, people wouldn't settle down to allow the president the floor. Shop owners were livid, bed-and-breakfast owners were scared. Were they next? After the fire at the Inn, many hotels worried and watched for their places to be targeted.

"Order," Doug said. "Let's have quiet so we can proceed with this meeting."

Everyone took their seats. The meeting was being hosted by the Old Stone Inn. Appetizers and wine were being served, and consumed, especially the wine. AsI looked over the crowd, I knew that they should have begun serving the wine after the meeting itself. This was a restless angry group.

"The first order of business is…"

"To find and bring in the firebug," Les Martin

shouted, his nose big and red.

Murmurs ran through the crowd.

"Sorry we're late," Erich said as he and Iris stepped through the old wooden door and took seats along the aisle.

Doug nodded, fear showing in the sweat dripping from his bald head.

"We have been watching the shops, our homes, and the town in shifts. Nothing has been reported. Who is this guy?" Les railed.

I looked around. Eyes were upon Erich. The sheriff was not present. He was not a brave man. We could not tell the association their plan to trap the arsonist/murderer, but we had to say something. He stood, "It has been a difficult case, but soon St. Michaels will be back to normal,"

"Normal!" one man accused. "My shop is a charred mess. There is nothing normal about our lives, our once beautiful town.

Doug whistled loud enough to stop a boat. "This is a trying time for all of us. It is not Erich's fault this is happening. He is here to help solve this mystery. Do not attack the man who we pray will settle this thing. We have other business to address. We will persevere although it is difficult to believe right now."

Whispers and sighs filled the room. I watched each person with a reporter's eye. Most seemed average, but filled with emotions they could not deal with for much longer. A few seemed closed off, and then there was the man in the corner, hat cocked to the side. Smirk in his eyes.

I tried to keep one eye on him throughout the evening without being noticed. Neither Dave nor Marley showed up. I hoped they were together— that Marley had gone home. Although her husband was flawed, my gut told me he was no criminal. But then, who did Knapps see?

When you lose your mind, where does it go? Looking into the old faded mirror he was pretty sure that is what has happened. Loneliness, too much time thinking negative thoughts, allowing paranoia to set in. Always thinking people are laughing at the lonely one, not realizing no one realized the sinking. Sure, the wife cared on a superficial daylight level. Was greeted at the Post Office, that kind of thing. But no one really listened, was privy to these innermost thoughts. Guessed that is why people went to see a psychiatrist or psychologist. Felt they were paying people just to listen to them vent, to ramble. They didn't have to make sense at all. Never had to heal or make progress as a person, find strength. Just tell the listener how they have been doing since the last session.

People who are understood rarely end up incarcerated. They feel whole. They have no monkey on their back scratching at their brains saying, "Is this all your life is about?"

For years they have a routine, friends who they talk with, pride. Do not hold in the intensities. Instead of expensive psychics and psychologists, someone should open a business called, "The Listener." Just sit there and listen a while. Ten minutes for twenty dollars.

I had showed up in town at a time when things were peaking. Started a newspaper. Made a star out of the "Firebug." An unknown star. Amazing that no one seemed to know who it is. Everyone was worried. "Who do you think would do it?" People asked everyday. Many agreed it was someone we knew, but also felt it was someone reclusive. Couldn't be anyone talking to them over coffee. Hard to imagine anyone with that much nerve!

But now Erich and I were possibly on to something. The culprit had been so careful. Wore a hat, gloves, face cover, left no trace. It could be anyone, really. But it wasn't just anyone.

Knapps and I moved things into the newly remodeled shop across from the Bank of America. A newspaper shop. Just what this town needs. Why would anyone move into a shop in St. Michaels with everything burning to the ground? Mountain girls are brave, and foolish, I thought.

Trying to make sense of things in my mind throughout the day I realized that they could quit now and just keep on with life and no one would ever know who it was.

But I was feeling damn lucky. Looking around, St. Michaels was quiet when it was just the locals, but the tourist trade brought some interesting people their way. Made things not so boring. Not so boring at all.

I'd always felt that there was something important to do in this life. Something that would be in the history books. So here is history in the making. And articles and at least one book to be written. I pushed a file cabinet into the door of my new office. I looked up as a sign was being hung. It said, "Bay Publishing & Investigations." Investigations? What did that mean? Was I in business with the P. I. and didn't even know it? What gives? This changed everything. Knapps shook his head, shrugged.

"Don't worry, it'll fit," Knapps said.
"Yeah, if we push the file cabinets together and set the bookshelves next to each other on the wall behind it. I think you're right."
Erich showed up and he and Knapps moved the heavy oak desk to the area I pointed to while I shoved file cabinets into place. The men watched as I ripped open boxes and filled the cabinets in quick order.
"Slow down," Erich said. "We have plenty of time."
"How do you know? The arsonist could be filling up his gas can to come after me right now!" I said.
"And who said we were a company? You have some nerve, Kojack."
"I'm sorry. I should have told you. I forgot. It's just part of the set-up. Relax."
"Relax? What Set-up?" Knapps asked. Knapps had gotten a haircut. Short and sort of preppy looking. He looked like a new kid.
Erich ignored the question and waved him to the

truck that was backed up to the door. They unloaded the rest of the boxes in silence with Knapps visibly fuming. Erich nodded to Jerry who was finishing up the apartment upstairs. He had put a security deposit on it for his own office, I discovered. Baltimore seems to have lost its mystery for him all of a sudden. There were no P.I.'s here that I knew of. It seemed to be a wide open field. I decided we could share the sign to make it more interesting, but was shook at his audacity and all it conjured. People were already stopping in nosing around. We were the talk of the town. No one could believe we had the nerve to rent space when the arsonist still ran loose. Something had to be done to get this guy to trip up, though. Erich couldn't have him outsmarting him in front of the whole Eastern Shore. I knew he wanted me to see him in action. To be proud I loved him. Did I? Enough to share that sign?

I hoped the action would not get violent-that no one would get hurt. The sheriff was ready to set up his deputies in strategic hiding places so that things went smoothly. It was time to shake this squirrel out of its tree. I was talking to the crowd that gathered on the sidewalk in front of the shop. They couldn't believe that they were getting a writer and a gumshoe moving into their boring little burgh.

"Believe it," Knapps mumbled trying to get his desk set up among the chaos.

As Erich sat the last box down in the back room he noticed Andy lurking around the truck. He watched him without his knowledge. Knapps watched him watch the old man and shook his head. He didn't see how that old bony grouch could be a suspect. He just didn't see it in his eyes, his stature, or his walk. Knapps liked to watch people's eyes. That's where you discovered who they are. Erich stepped outside and whistled, startling the old man. He jumped a bit, turned to see who was bothering him. "Can I help you with something?"

"No!" he barked and sauntered away at an easy pace.

Erich watched him.

CHAPTER 21

Geese were honking overhead so loud that they woke me. Erich and I had fallen asleep fully clothed in each others arms. A quick steak on the boat's grill, a couple glasses of wine, and we laid on the bed to talk. Moving into the office must have worn us out. It was 4 A. M. according to my watch. I pulled away from him trying not to disturb his solid slumber.

On deck I stretched and ran my fingers through my messy hair. I decided to walk home to take Hank out. He must be frantic! Unless Iris took him out, he had been holding it since four the day before. As I jumped onto the dock I noticed no lights on any boats. Not even the big one. It was funny, even with the reward we offered, no real leads fell in our laps. I decided to go by the Post Office and get a paper to read with my coffee. Main Street was quiet. Eerily so. My new office looked deserted, so I went there first. Upon unlocking the door, I found it was already open. My heart thumped in my chest. My knees shook, but I pushed the door open anyway. A note lay on my desk written in a shaky hand.

"I know what you are doing!"

I turned on the lights and saw Knapps sleeping in his chair, head on the desk. I shook him, showed him the note.

"I didn't see anyone," he said rubbing his eyes and shaking his head.

"What are you doing here?"

"I must have sat down for a moment and never got up. Sorry."

I led him out of the building and locked up after looking around. No one was in sight. We walked to Iris's house together. He splashed water in his face and left for the boat. Oyster dredging today and he was late.

I got the leash on my jumping dog and ran up the road after setting up the coffee pot to run while I was gone. I went back to the office, but this time sat in darkness myself to see if anything would happen. At 5 A.M. Hank yipped. It was Andy going upstairs to clean up. He didn't even look our way.

I decided it was getting light out and no one would be sneaking around then, so I took off down the back street to home. There I ran right into Dave. He looked drawn.

"My God, you scared me!" I said.

"Sorry. Can't sleep lately."

I ran back home and Iris was up taking Ralph out.

Dogs seemed to run our lives. Something was scratching at the back of my mind. I had to run more to clear my head, so I headed down toward the Mt. Pleasant area along the water. It was usually very quiet there in the morning. Hank loved to run. Thoughts swirled around my head until one came through and stopped me. Just then a cloud burst and drenched us to the bones.

Later, Iris was at the library where she spent a lot of her spare time. Erich had called earlier berating me for going off on my own. I told him to be careful. Ralph let me know he was ready to come in with a big "WOOF!" He shook on the porch and curled up on his big dog bed in the corner, gave a huge sigh and fell asleep. No problem for him to sleep no matter what went on in the world. Hank, on the other hand, hated storms. He was prancing and pawing at me, trying to make me understand that storms are not to be taken lightly. He cried to enlist my help in stopping the thunder and crashing lightning that landed so close. I found a flashlight and some candles and matches in case we lost power.

Being home alone with the dogs was a welcome relief to the chaos of trying to flesh out this firebug/murderer who walked the streets among us. I was not really afraid. I knew I should be, but I was too tired. Today my mind and spirit were in dire need of recharging. Hank ran under the table when the lightening cracked in the yard in front of the porch. Ralph barely opened his eyes, then everything went black. I lit the many candles throughout the house, several in each room. It gave me a soothing feeling, unlike when the power went out in the middle of a deep freeze in Pennsylvania. Freezing to death never appealed to me. I had a propane fireplace for the old place, and it kept things plenty cozy during snow storms that knocked power out for days at a time, sometimes weeks. Seemed worlds away, decades away rather than weeks. Now I was in the midst of the Eastern Shore of the Chesapeake Bay rebuilding my business, my life. Hank cried under the table, but wouldn't come out no matter how I coaxed him. Treats were not worth it, his eyes told me. He looked at me as if I was crazy not to be hiding under there with him. Maybe I was.

Ah, there is nothing like a good storm to get my people's nerves raw. The power was still out. The sky was ferocious looking with its black fast moving clouds. Trees whipped sideways. The town was pitch dark. Candles flickered through a few shades and curtains, but for the most part, St. Michaels was huddled inside praying for the sun to rise and bring them another perfect day in paradise. A paradise charred.

Moving along the alleys my office building stood silent. Newly painted yellow with dusty blue shutters, it looked like a beach house. Who did I think I was, thinking I could save the town?

Thoughts bounced around my head. Keep control. This is important. Keep the pace. Unrecognizable in navy foul weather gear, everyone looked alike wearing the same thing in weather like this around the Bay. Navy or yellow, take your pick.

For a few moments, no one stirred on Talbot Street. A siren went off just then. Trucks flew through town ignoring the crosswalks. A person could be killed trying to get to the other side. Wouldn't that be an irony?

Anxiety filled me. My rubber boots squished on the pavement. I looked like a waterman out in this weather. No one would know it was me.

With my chin to my chest, I pushed forward against the wind and pelting rain. I could see where I was going by the ground.

I was dry under the rain gear when I pushed the key into the lock. I stood in the doorway listening. It was eerie being there in the dark storm. I hung my coat on the brass peg and it dripped on the newly shined tile. Sitting at my desk I saw nothing out the windows but rain.

"You shouldn't be out in this weather," he said smiling at me from under the dark rubber hood.

The dripping water on the tile floor seemed so loud now. Drip, drip, drip. So did my heart thumping like the thunder Hank ran from. Had he been waiting for me? I leaned onto my desk to give a nonchalant air to my ragged nerves. Anxiety threatened to buckle my knees. Gasoline fumes now began to float thick in the closed up room. I needed anger to replace the incessant fear that was making me sweat, shake. I took several deep breaths while holding his eyes, but the fumes were sickening me. "Why are you here? Do you have your ad for the paper? How did you get in?"

"Door was unlocked, Sherlock. I saw the gun in his gloved hand.

"You're the firebug? YOU??" I asked holding tight to the desk where I now sat. "Didn't you grow up with Agnes? Wasn't she your wife's friend?"

"Doesn't make you feel too safe now, does it?"

"How does it make you feel?"

"Not as good as I had hoped."

"Why the hell are you telling me?"

"You just don't know."

"Tell me a story," I smirked, disgusted. "I have time, I think."

His head jerked when lightening struck just outside the back door. I never took my eyes off of him, but still held onto the edge of my solid oak desk, like it was a life preserver.

"He approached me and I lifted my arms for him to see they were empty. I was wearing form fitting cotton knit lounging clothes under the rain gear. He could see there was no weapon on me. His Cheshire cat grin gave me a chill up my spine.

"Tell me something, would you? I am a naturally curious person. Most writers are. Why burn all those buildings if you just wanted to get rid of the competition? Doesn't wash."

"Competition? It is not that way. I always liked fire, in women, in the hearth, the flames are an amazing aphrodisiac. You should try it." He laughed out loud. "You'll see, though, won't you? At first I really just wanted to burn my inn and rebuild…or take the money and travel. I wasn't really sure. I never set a fire before, not in a building, so I started looking things up on the internet and thought I'd try it out on one of the stores since there were shop owners I wouldn't mind seeing squirm.

"Did Agnes find out?"

"Shut up!"

"Look, you might as well tell me. Hell, the only time I met her was when she was dying in that shop. Thanks a lot for placing that in my mind for life, by the way."

"Welcome," he nodded. "I have a question for you. Where is your night in shining armor? You two have been flaunting yourselves around St. Michaels like the king and queen. The reporter and the P.I. This ain't make-believe, girl. Some investigator Mr. Wonderful turned out to be!"

"Is that what this is about? You've always been jealous of him, haven't you?

"God, you're nosy, but it was easier than you'd imagine, fooling him and all of you."

"I'll bet," I mumbled.

"He reached out to slap me. I saw it coming and dove across the desk knocking him to the ground. As he flicked the lighter and flames sprang from the

newspaper on the floor, I kicked him in the chest
and threw my jacket over the small fire. Whew,
what an odor—rubber burning.

Erich walked in the back door soaked. Lightening
rocked the office, lit us up. "Doug?" he gave us
both a sad smirk. "Nice work, the false fire alarm,"
he said shaking his hanging head.

He crouched down to look at Doug and pulled him
up roughly. "What happened to you? What the hell
are you doing torturing everyone? Randy will never
get over losing Agnes!" He shook the man hard.

"Easy Sherlock," Doug said, an empty look in his
eyes.

"Agnes found him out. The rest was for his
entertainment." I informed him. "It's over now." I
handed him the 22 caliber pistol the town's council
President had been holding to intimidate me.

"Not for him, it's not. Not for our Fire Chief."

"Cedar?" Knapps mumbled as he rubbed his eyes.
Must have fallen asleep upstairs.

"That's my sidekick," I smiled as Erich led Doug
out through the storm and across the street to the
sheriff's office."

"Welcome to the Eastern Shore," he said, kissing
me on the forehead on his way out my door.

The streets were still quiet. No one realized what
had happened while they sat in candlelight awaiting
the electric company to repair their lines.

"Why? Why would you kill my Agnes?"

"You weren't the only one who loved her," was all

he said. He had been mostly silent these past two days. His lawyer was hired by his wife who stood by his side praying. She brought him clean clothes. Before they moved him to the county lock-up pending tests and paper work, he let them know that he did not set the fire at the video store.

I opened up the new office the very next day. Moved all my belongings to the upstairs. Erich agreed to give up the space so I could use it as an apartment. He could work from the boat easy enough. I could not give up that much of myself so quickly, but was enjoying seeing him. Knapps seemed older somehow. I had been in St. Michaels for one month to the day. Walking Hank to the water, I waved to the guys on the liar's bench, but didn't feel like talking. The town buzzed with gossip. Something that never affected me. Was used to it where I came from. Small towns.

I could see the big yacht leaving the harbor. Hank howled all of a sudden. A deep breath, a long look at the sky, the water, and it was time to finish that novel. Not the ending I imagined, but this little village was humming away again. People could cut their grass without being under suspicion. Andy could be his grumpy self and no one took exception. Buildings were being reconstructed. That charred smell was washed away in the storm.

Fall in St. Michaels was upon us, and it was time to concentrate on my happiness. To live, to write, to love. I said goodbye to Willie. Knew he would always watch over his mother. Knew now that it was not my fault. I could never have known the cook was that crazy. Just like Doug, St. Michaels', ex President of the town council, he was an actor of the best quality. But I did learn one thing about this type of crazy. It's common.

ABOUT THE AUTHOR

Marci Lynn McGuinness is the author of 28 books, several screen plays, and dozens of articles. She is a regional history and auto racing columnist for the *Herald Standard* newspaper, and a storyteller, extraordinaire.

The southwestern Pennsylvania native is presently developing an annual booklet, *Laurel Highland Legends*, and a mystery, *Murder in the Vineyard*.

Contact: shorepublications@yahoo.com
www.ohiopyle.info
www.uniontownspeedway.com
www.amazon.com/author/marcimcguinness